Would Amber sacrifice her innocence for a once-in-a-lifetime opportunity?

"I suppose you know that Gina will be offered the contract if you refuse to sign. . . She's flying in tonight from New York. . . Tomorrow she expects to be told whether Len wants her for the new campaign, or whether he's signed. . .a new model."

Amber lifted her chin. "Then tell her the contract is hers. I made my decision before you brought me here." She could feel the sparks shooting from her eyes.

For a moment he didn't respond. Then a slow grin split his face. He looked ridiculously boyish. "You're irresistible when you're angry, you know." His expression shifted, and something unfamiliar flickered in his eyes. . . "You may not be a model. And today you're not a secretary. But you *are*. . .a very desirable woman."

She was suddenly aware of his nearness—the massive shoulders, the bare chest, the strong jawline. She could not look away. A storm of emotion swirled inside her. Like the strong ocean currents, she felt herself drawn into the undertow. She was helpless. . .powerless

Almost against his will, it seemed, Anton backed away. "But then. . .Ken, is it? is the one true love of your life . . .and you've never gotten over him. . . You're either a true innocent or you're playing a very convincing game. And not even *I* can decide which it is."

"I don't play games, Mr. Pasetti" . . . How could she be so ambivalent—despising him one minute, wanting him to crush her in his arms the next? . . .

"Oh, I think you may be playing the most dangerous game of your life. Gina says you're determined to be more than my secretary. . . She thinks you want to be. . .my *wife*."

YVONNE LEHMAN, an award-winning novelist, lives in the heart of the Smoky Mountains, with her husband. They are the parents of four grown children. In addition to being an inspirational romance writer, she is also the founder of the Blue Ridge Christian Writers' Conference.

A Whole New World

Yvonne Lehman

Heartsong Presents

To Cindy and David
Two beautiful people—inside and out

A note from the Author:
I love to hear from my readers! You may write to me at the following address: **Yvonne Lehman**
Author Relations
P.O. Box 719
Uhrichsville, OH 44683

All scripture quotations, unless otherwise indicated, are taken from the HOLY BIBLE, NEW INTERNATIONAL VERSION®. NIV®. Copyright © 1973, 1978, 1984 by International Bible Society. Used by permission of Zondervan Publishing House. All rights reserved.

ISBN 1-55748-969-6

A WHOLE NEW WORLD

Cover illustration by Randy Hamlin.

PRINTED IN THE U.S.A.

one

Amber Jennings, what are you doing here?

Amber groaned inwardly as she stepped inside the plushly carpeted reception room of the Pasetti Modeling Agency, San Diego's finest. It didn't help to settle her nerves that the receptionist was a stunning blond, her flaxen hair pulled back in a sophisticated chignon, looking as if she herself had stepped off the pages of some fashion magazine.

"What can we do for you?" the young woman asked when Amber approached the desk. At closer range, she could see that the woman's eyes—an unusual tawny gold, flecked with green—were dancing. Empathy. . .or amusement? Amber couldn't be sure.

The smile was sincere enough, though. "Do you have an appointment?"

"I believe the employment office called. I'm Amber Jennings. . .here about the secretarial job you advertised in the classifieds."

The receptionist, whose nameplate read LYNN, ran a tapered, polished nail down a list, then looked up. "Mr. Pasetti will see you shortly. Just have a seat."

Amber settled herself on a cream-colored leather couch, trying to ignore the whole flight of butterflies that took off in her stomach. She couldn't help staring at the blond, now taking a telephone call. She was wearing a

5

bone-colored dress, set off by gold earrings and choker. Glancing around her, Amber could see that everything in the room—low-slung sofas arranged around glass-topped tables—was some tone of gold or ivory. Except for the greens, of course. Potted palms, ficus trees, and hanging baskets of lush greenery brought in a touch of the outdoors. Amber looked down at her good navy suit—the best thing she owned—and cringed. This place was like nothing she had ever seen back home in North Carolina. In these elegant surroundings, she stuck out like a sore thumb.

Catching herself drumming her fingers nervously on her purse, she laid it aside, picked up a magazine from a table, and began to leaf through. This issue featured some of the high-fashion Pasetti models, and feeling a fresh wave of anxiety, Amber threw down the magazine and picked up her purse again, fiddling with the clasp. This was just not going to work. She ought to cancel her appointment and leave right now, before she had to face the embarrassment of hearing, "Don't call us. We'll call you!"

At that moment, an attractive brunette entered the office and spoke to the receptionist loudly enough for Amber to hear. So she wasn't the *only* person applying for this job!

The petite young woman sank into a seat near Amber and offered a forced smile. Apparently too excited to sit still, she jumped to her feet and proceeded to pace the room. In her high heels and flame red dress, the other applicant made Amber feel even more plain vanilla than she had before.

Still, in business school, she had been taught that first impressions were important, and choosing one's interview outfit could make or break your chances of landing a job. Navy, she had learned, signified stability, diligence, and perseverance. That's why she'd decided on this conservative suit and simple white blouse. Still, maybe the instructor hadn't had in mind a fancy job with a modeling agency!

Now the brunette was studying the photographs on the walls, and Lynn rose to explain. For the first time, Amber noticed that the gorgeous receptionist was very, very pregnant. Could it be *her* job someone would be filling?

Overhearing her explanation of the photos, Amber recalled her own year with an advertising agency back home. She knew something about such layouts, which often focused on a single physical feature—a hand displaying a ring, a foot modeling a shoe, even a perfectly formed ear studded with a diamond or other precious stone. Although she recognized the concept, she also realized that these photos were much more sophisticated than others she had seen. The Pasetti Agency obviously catered to the elite publications.

There's a place for both, Amber told herself resolutely, resisting again the impulse to bolt from the room and forget the whole thing.

A closed door near Lynn's desk bore the name ANTON PASETTI in gold letters. The door opened, and another tall blond exited. After a brief assessment of Amber and the brunette, she stopped by the desk. "He asked me to wa-a-ait." She closed her eyes dreamily and sighed.

Lynn gave a knowing smile. "He's probably checking your references. Good luck."

Still in a daze, the blond nodded and drifted to a chair across the room.

Well, so much for that, Amber decided. The woman had probably already landed the job. In fact, she could be a model herself, with that great bone structure set off by arched brows and silver-blond hair. She'd fit right in. Even her color scheme was right.

Self-consciously, Amber put her hand to her own hair. She had pulled it back, pinned it into a simple twist, and fastened it with a barrette. The color, a dark brown, was far from spectacular. In fact, her only decent feature was her eyes, and even they were just a little more than "run-of-the-mill," she decided, lapsing into one of the quaint expressions she often heard in her part of the Tarheel State. Some folks had said she was pretty, but she'd never believed them. All she could remember were those miserable preteen years when her eyes and mouth had been too big for her face.

As a Christian, though, she'd never relied too much on her looks. As her grandmother had always said, "Pretty is as pretty does," which was Aunt Sophie's rough translation of 1 Samuel 16:7: "Man looks at the outward appearance, but the Lord looks at the heart." Still, to be surrounded by all this feminine perfection was a little daunting.

"Mr. Pasetti is *so* good-looking," the tall blond gushed, giving Amber just another sharp reminder that some people didn't share her views.

"And single, too," Lynn said in a loud whisper from behind her hand. "Oh, excuse me." She responded to the low beep on her intercom, pressed a button, and listened. "Yes, sir. I'll tell her." She leaned forward. "Jan, Mr. Pasetti thinks you have beautiful hands," the blond gasped and appeared ready to faint, Amber thought, "but not for typing." Lynn hastened to add, "If you're interested, he'd like to use your hands for a layout."

"My hands?" She held them up in front of her as if they

were not attached, then blinked. "Well...sure! I mean...of course! I've always wanted to be a model!"

Lynn nodded. No doubt she'd heard that line before, Amber concluded.

The brunette closed her eyes. Amber couldn't help thinking she was probably praying that she'd get lucky, too. *If she does, then maybe I'd have a chance at the secretarial job, after all.* Lynn had to call her name twice before the message sank in. "Amber Jennings, you may go in now."

Amber took a deep breath and rose, dropping her purse, then bumping into a table in her effort to retrieve it. Feeling like a klutz, she made her way to the door with the gold lettering, turned the brass knob, and stepped inside.

There was time for only a glimpse of the room and the man behind the desk when suddenly she was blinded by a beam of southern California sunshine streaming through the undraped window at his back. She could barely make out his tall silhouette—with very broad shoulders—standing to greet her. She squinted and turned her face from the light.

"Sorry," he apologized in a deep baritone voice, "I didn't expect that sudden burst of splendor. The sky has been overcast all day." He turned and released the raised miniblinds, then adjusted them to keep the golden rays at bay. "I confess I'd rather be outdoors than in, and far from the city, I might add. San Diego is like a concrete jungle, and the eighth floor of this building is not much better than a cage in the zoo. Much too confining."

As he spoke, head turned, she took in his striking appearance—muscular build, dark hair curling at the collar, strong profile. Everyone had said he was handsome. But she hadn't been prepared for. . .*this!*

He turned to find her staring openly, and to cover her confusion, she plunged in before he could initiate the interview. "Confining?" She gave a wry laugh. "My entire cottage would fit into this one room!"

"That's quite a southern drawl you have there."

Was he mocking her? "Well, I'm not surprised. I've lived in the South all my life. . .actually in only one small town in the South."

He picked up some papers from his desk and flipped through them. "Swanna. . .how do you pronounce the name of the place?"

"Swan-na-no-a," Amber sounded it out for him. "It's a small town in western North Carolina."

"Never heard of it." He looked up from the file folder in his hands. "What does it mean?"

Despite the fact that Swannanoa had been home for all of her twenty-two years, she really didn't know. But she wasn't about to admit it. "I've. . .heard two different stories," she said uneasily. "Some say it means 'pleasant valley,' while others say it means 'pig path.' "

"Pig. . . ?" She could see him struggling to suppress a smile before coughing into his hand.

"Actually," she went on miserably, just wanting to get this over with, "I think it's probably named for an Indian chief."

"Then you have some Indian blood?"

The only person who had ever mentioned such a thing was Aunt Sophie. "I think my father's father had a smidgen of Cherokee in him."

He nodded, studying her intently, as if she were a painting in a museum. . .or a bug under glass. "That. . .er

...smidgen,' " this time the smile crept through, "no doubt accounts for the cheekbones and the vivid coloring—especially those eyes."

While she was trying to figure out if he was pleased or displeased with the possibility, he read from the application form: "Amber Elizabeth Jennings?"

"That's right," she answered politely.

"And I'm Anton Pasetti." The lilt of that deep resonant voice gave the sound of music to his name. "Have a seat, please." He gestured toward the chair beside his desk.

While he glanced over the application form, Amber twisted the clasp on her purse. He looked her way when she clicked it shut. Feeling foolish, she slid the small handbag out of sight, then folded her hands together on her lap, making sure that her skirt fell demurely just above her knees. *And remember not to cross your legs,* she could hear her instructor say. Instead, she slanted them properly—in the parallel position.

She knew it had been only a very few minutes since she'd entered the room, but it was beginning to feel like forever. She tried to concentrate on the room. Here, too, the decor was in neutral tones, with photos on the walls. Unlike the reception room, this one was dominated by Mr. Pasetti's desk of polished cherry. Triple the size of a normal executive desk, this one could easily accommodate large portfolios and photo spreads.

She had been told that there were two job openings and that Anton Pasetti would be interviewing those applying for the position of his personal secretary/receptionist. Amber had felt qualified for either. Now, she wasn't so sure this was the job for her. For some reason she couldn't fathom, this man made her feel distinctly uncomfortable.

"You worked with an advertising agency in North Carolina," he said, glancing briefly at her.

She nodded. Just as she was beginning to relax a little, something on the form caught his attention, and he lifted his eyebrows. "You had *two* promotions within a year?" He leaned back, swiveling his chair to peer at her quizzically.

Feeling warm, Amber put her hand to the high neck of her blouse, then abruptly dropped it to her lap. *Don't let them see you sweat!* came to mind. She was aware that she didn't sparkle like the brunette outside, nor was she the cool and collected type, like the blond. Close scrutiny would tell him she was just a small-town girl. But she was a good secretary, and the advertising agency in Asheville, although small, was quite successful.

All the information was right there in front of him, on her resumé. But she suspected he wanted to hear her version of the facts. Still, it was probably best not to mention that the owner of the ad agency was also the uncle of her former fiancé. "I graduated from a reputable business school, Mr. Pasetti," she said, plunging in. "After that, I worked for the agency for a year."

He swiveled the chair back to the desk and covered the papers with a large hand. "You worked there a year," he echoed, "took a three-month leave of absence, then returned to the agency for three months?" Leaning forward, he propped his forearms on the desk. "Weren't you happy with your work, Miss Jennings?"

"My leave of absence had nothing to do with the work," she said quickly. *Careful, Amber, don't sound so defensive.* She shook her head slightly and stared at the window, where the stubborn sun trickled through the blinds, spearing her in the angle of its beam, but casting Anton Pasetti into the shadows. She wished she could disappear as easily. But the spotlight was on her, his penetrating gaze probing memories, emotions she had no desire to explore.

She had come here, to this fascinating land of sea and sun, to escape what had happened. But right now this disturbing man was making that impossible. Shifting her gaze to him again, Amber looked across the wide expanse of desk at the man frowning down at her application. She noticed the determined thrust of his jawline, softened by a slight indentation in his chin. Funny. She'd never thought much about chins before. But his was different. Was it that the dimple made him appear less intimidating, more vulnerable? Boyish, even? She focused on the dimple. Anything to get this interview behind her.

After a moment of awkward silence, she realized that *he* was focusing on her *hands,* clenched in her lap.

"You're engaged to be married?" he asked brusquely, his eyes locked on the diamond ring on her third finger, left hand.

Heart racing, she looked down. She'd forgotten to take it off! How could she have been so careless? She'd meant to remove the ring as soon as she arrived in California, but had never found the proper moment, nor the proper place to keep something so significant. In the meantime it had felt perfectly natural on her finger. Now it was too late. And any explanation she might try to make would sound lame.

"You're engaged?" he asked for the second time.

"Yes." She felt the hot color flood her face at the lie. "That is. . .I mean. . .no." She shook her head helplessly.

"It's. . .really hard to explain, Mr. Pasetti."

Anton Pasetti turned in the swivel chair to face her directly, apparently annoyed. "I'm not trying to be personal, Miss Jennings. It's just that I'd prefer not to hire someone who might soon marry and leave us."

"Oh, I have no intention of marrying," she blurted out, and, seeing the sudden question in his eyes, amended, "that is. . .not now. I'm only interested in my career."

A comprehending sneer curled the corners of his mouth. "Ah, your career. A secretarial career, I take it."

Amber's chin went up, and she met his gaze head on. "That's the job I'm applying for, Mr. Pasetti."

"Yes." He hunched his shoulders. "But I also know—from experience—that most applicants have their sights set on modeling."

Amber momentarily forgot her uneasiness. "Well, _I_ have no such illusions, I can assure you. We both know I could never be a model."

His eyebrows shot up and the cynicism settled about his lips again. "And why not, Miss Jennings?" he asked, looking at her nose. Was there a smudge on it?

Distracted, she shifted in her chair. "I'm not tall enough."

At that remark, he threw back his head and laughed heartily. But his laughter didn't bother her nearly as much as the boldly assessing gaze that swept her from head to toe. She didn't know what this man wanted, but apparently it wasn't a secretary; it was a _target_ for all that bitterness and frustration that crackled in the atmosphere around him!

He cleared his throat and drew his brows together in a frown. But the arrogant grin belied his fierce look. "Height isn't everything in the modeling business. Certain products don't require that a model be tall. . . ." He paused, then added with a twinkle in his eyes that she now realized were not black, but a smoky gray. He nodded meaningfully toward her hand. "Engagement rings, for instance."

Amber gasped at the implication. He must be thinking she'd worn the ring to call attention to her hands! She determined to hold her tongue and get out of there as soon as possible.

Anton Pasetti glanced at her nose again, then turned calmly to study the papers in front of him. His tone was entirely professional as he continued. "There are plenty of executives who would give their eyeteeth for a woman whose ambition is to be a secretary these days."

Fortunately, before she could say she had all the eyeteeth she needed, he pushed a button on his desk phone and asked Lynn to get the North Carolina advertising agency on the phone. He gave the name and address Amber had written on the form, then glanced at her, his gaze again lingering on her nose.

Just as she put her hand to her face, he warned, "Don't do that. You'll make it peel." He chuckled. "You really should be more careful in the sun. A pink nose detracts from your best feature. . .your eyes."

Flustered, she didn't know whether to thank him for the compliment or punch him in his own perfect nose! But his next words dispelled any notion that he had intended to flatter her.

"Aren't you rather warm?" He scanned her long-sleeved suit and the white blouse buttoned all the way to the collar.

By now her flaming cheeks must surely match her nose. "I. . .I haven't had an opportunity to buy any new clothes yet. It's still wintertime in North Carolina in March. And, as you mentioned, it was cool and overcast here this morning."

"Mmm. Well, at least the suit's in good taste. . .for a secretary."

Not your *secretary!* she considered flinging back at him. *No way would I want to work for you!* In a few short moments, he had managed to insult her home town, humiliate her, and render her speechless. He obviously was the kind of man who dominated those around him.

After everything that had happened, she needed new experiences, new friends, a fresh start. Until now, she had felt the Lord had led her here. . .to heal. But now she was beginning to wonder if she had heard Him correctly. She certainly didn't fit into the fast-paced, flashy California lifestyle. . .much less the office of the impossible Anton Pasetti!

two

"Mr. Jackson," Anton Pasetti's voice broke into Amber's silent monologue.

While he chatted with her former employer over the phone, she took stock of her situation. She really had to find a job soon, before her carefully hoarded funds ran out. Maybe she ought to reconsider. . .that is, if there was a chance in the world she'd be offered a position here. She eyed Mr. Pasetti's strong profile, trying to gauge his mood. What was Mr. Jackson telling him? She'd been assured that Ken's uncle would put in a good word for her. He'd even been the one who had suggested she contact the Pasetti Agency as soon after arriving in San Diego as possible. Mr. Jackson, "Uncle Jack," as he'd insisted she call him after her engagement to his nephew, "had hired her on at his small ad agency and had praised her efficiency and creativity.

She darted another glance at Mr. Pasetti. He was frowning again.

He swiveled slowly in the brown leather chair, turning his back on her. Uncle Jack must be telling him about the accident. Well, she had come over two thousand miles to escape that very thing. She *had* to get out of here.

Amber jumped to her feet and was moving toward the door when a rumbling baritone halted her in her tracks. "Miss Jennings," he called in an irritated tone, "would you

17

mind very much if we finished this interview?"

Reluctantly, Amber returned to her chair and perched on the edge, not daring to look him in the eye. If he mentioned Ken, she'd scream.

"Well, that's that," Mr. Pasetti said. Good. It would soon be over. "Mr. Jackson gave you an excellent recommendation. Superior, in fact." He hesitated before going on. "Normally our applicants come here with their well-written resumés, their beautiful faces, and their lips literally dripping honey. It's refreshing to have a genuine secretary apply. You did say you had no aspirations at all to be a model?"

She knew by his tone of voice that he didn't believe her. Giving him a level look, she spoke as positively as she knew how. "As I've already told you, I haven't the slightest interest in modeling."

He drummed his fingers on the desktop. "Then are you really that unaware of your own potential?"

It sounded like a trick question. Well, she was tired of his games. She squared her shoulders and stood once again, keeping her mouth shut before she said something they'd both regret.

In one fluid movement, he was on his feet, hand extended. Puzzled, she allowed his brief, firm handshake.

"Welcome to the agency, Miss Jennings."

"Wel. . . ?" Her eyes widened and she blinked in surprise. Then she narrowed her gaze. Was that sympathy she detected in his expression? She felt a stab of resentment and something like guilt. Anton Pasetti was the last man on earth she would have chosen to know about her past. But there was little doubt that Uncle Jack had told him. If so, Pasetti was probably giving her the job because he felt sorry for her. Maybe he figured her heart was broken.

On the other hand, Anton Pasetti hadn't really seemed very interested in her one way or the other but only in hiring a capable secretary. Just for an instant she felt a twinge of envy. Unlike the blond and the brunette in the reception room, she was far from model material. But what difference did that make? She had the job for which she was most qualified. As for Mr. Pasetti, she'd do her job, but she'd do her best to steer clear of him as much as possible. Like oil and water, their personalities just didn't mix.

"Tell the other applicants they may leave, Lynn," he was saying into the intercom. "And take Miss Jennings to Charis."

❧

Lynn had a cocky grin on her face when Amber returned and they were alone in the reception room. "I had a feeling you'd be the one to get the job."

"Really? What gave you that idea?"

"You didn't swoon over the photos, the magazines," she glanced toward her boss's door and dropped her voice, "nor, apparently, over Mr. Pasetti."

"Oh. And *I* thought I was hired because of my qualifications."

"That, too," Lynn admitted, hoisting herself out of her chair to shake Amber's hand. "Congratulations."

"Oh. . .and congratulations to *you*," she said, dropping her gaze to the expandable front of the receptionist's smart maternity dress.

Lynn gave her bulging tummy a fond pat. "Thanks. I've decided to stay home for a while with my children. My three-year-old has grown so fast that I don't want to miss any more of these early, formative years."

Amber nodded. "So yours is one of the positions open?" For the first time, it dawned on her that she hadn't been told which of the two positions she had been hired to fill.

"Yes. The other is at the opposite end of this floor. I'm to take you down there right now. Come on."

Lynn guided her down a long corridor and past several closed doors. Amber learned that the entire fifteen-story building was owned by Pasetti Enterprises, with several floors leased to other businesses. Anton Pasetti's penthouse apartment occupied the top floor.

The end of the hallway opened into a huge room, divided into cubicles. From there, another receptionist directed Lynn and Amber to an inner office.

Seated behind the desk was the most strikingly beautiful older woman Amber had ever seen. Silvery hair was swept back from her face in a dramatic short cut. Even when the corners of her eyes crinkled slightly with the welcoming smile that seemed to emanate from deep within, her beauty was only further enhanced. And when she stood to shake hands, Amber could see that the woman's figure was trim and toned. Her dark gray suit with a printed silk scarf at the neck was the perfect foil for vivid blue eyes that sparkled with warmth.

"Amber Jennings, this is Charis Lamarr, vice-president in charge of employee relations," Lynn introduced them.

"Call me Charis," she began as Lynn waved and left to return to her office. "With Lynn's second child arriving soon and one of my secretaries on permanent disability, we're in dire need of help around here."

"Oh, so I'll be working for *you!*" Amber felt a wave of relief wash over her. "I'm looking forward to it," she said with utter sincerity.

A look of mild surprise altered the woman's classic features. "Most women would jump at the chance to work for Anton," she flicked her gaze to Amber's left hand, "but I see you're engaged."

Amber felt her spirits take a dive. Why had she done this to herself—invite speculation? She took a deep breath. "My fiancé was killed several months ago."

"Oh, I *am* sorry." The blue eyes sparked with sympathy. "It must be very difficult for one so young to have experienced such a loss."

Amber was tempted to shrug the subject aside. But she supposed she should be honest and upfront with her new employer. "I wear the ring out of a sense of loyalty to Ken," she explained, "not because I can't accept the fact that he's dead."

The genuine concern in the older woman's expression prompted more of a confession than Amber had intended. "At first I tried to make some sense of the accident. But it seemed such a waste. I even blamed God for disrupting my plans. I know now it was He Who finally gave me the courage to accept Ken's death." Her pulse quickened as it always did when she shared her faith with a stranger.

Charis walked over to the window, her back to Amber for a moment. The sun had apparently disappeared behind the clouds again, lending a dismal quality to the room. Charis's voice was equally subdued when she spoke. "I know what you mean, Amber." Her shoulders heaved beneath the fine fabric of her suit.

"Then you're a Christian, too?" Amber asked hopefully.

The older woman turned then with a rueful smile. "A relatively new one," she admitted. "I'm still learning to trust the Lord. I had a dear friend whose example I'm trying to follow. She, like your fiancé, died young, and the closer she came to death, the more confident she was that God was with her." Her voice had taken on a tone of wonder. Then, with a wave of her hand, she dismissed the subject. "Perhaps we'll talk at another time. Right now," she went on, sitting erect and looking every inch the vice-president of a prestigious modeling agency, "let me explain how we get things done."

Amber listened intently as Charis explained the procedures. The company briefed all incoming staff on good grooming, makeup, poise, and etiquette.

"In short, a minimodeling course," Charis summarized.

Amber's momentary confusion gave way to dawning awareness. Of course. The tools of the trade. This agency's business was to obtain advertising contracts for its models, so all employees were expected to be well-informed. There was even a modeling school on the ninth and tenth floors, she was told.

Grooming, poise, etiquette. . . . While Charis talked on, Amber's thoughts strayed. She could sure use some tips in at least one of those areas. If she could just learn how to keep her cool. . .such as during that recent encounter with Mr. Pasetti. . .

She snapped her attention back to the present just in time to hear the last of the briefing before Charis stood to signal the end of the interview. "So, Amber, on Monday morning you'll begin your training period."

Amber felt her cheeks heat. Had she missed something while her thoughts wandered to the opposite end of the building? "Did you mention how long the training sessions will take?"

"It depends upon the person," Charis replied with a thoughtful look on her face. "We don't put our office staff through the same extensive training our models receive. But we do expect our employees to give customers an impression of the Pasetti look."

The Pasetti look. Flawless features, sleek figure, well-coiffed hair. In other words, physical perfection. What ordinary woman could possibly measure up? It was all so superficial.

Yet the women she'd met so far, Lynn and Charis, were much more than pretty faces. They were warm, caring people. And Charis, at least, was a Christian. Maybe glamour was not altogether incompatible with Christianity, so long as one's motives were right. Besides, it was a job in a field she knew well, although this time the advertisers would be selling something less tangible than tools or toothpaste. This time they would be selling a look: "the Pasetti look."

For a moment, recalling her earlier encounter with Anton Pasetti, Amber felt a stab of anxiety. But it passed quickly. At least, she wouldn't be working directly with Mr. Pasetti himself. She looked down at her engagement ring and was freshly reminded of her loss. . .and of his curious scrutiny.

She'd told her immediate superior the truth, so she didn't owe *him* a full explanation. But lest he suspect she was too frivolous, or worse, too irresponsible for a job with the agency, she'd continue wearing the ring for a while. She'd just have to postpone, for a little longer, making a complete break with the past. It certainly couldn't do any harm. Could it?

⁂

Amber steered her blue Escort out of San Diego, "the

concrete jungle," as Anton Pasetti had called it, and was soon speeding along the palm-lined freeway. Because it was not rush hour, the traffic moved quickly, matching her exhilaration at having landed a job, one that far exceeded any expectations she'd entertained that morning. Without having worked a single day, she had the distinct feeling that she would gain much more from the Pasetti Agency than she could ever give it.

Twenty minutes later she turned onto a smaller road, which led to the shopping center near her new home. She splurged on several items—a basket of ivy to hang in the kitchen window, a fern, and a couple of bright toss pillows for the living room—to add a personal touch to the cookie-cutter motor-court unit she had rented. She wouldn't buy any new clothes yet at least not until she consulted with Charis Lamarr as to the image she needed to project.

After parking beside the scraggly palm at the back of the cottage, she entered the small efficiency kitchen. The cottage was nothing special—only a living room, bedroom, and bath beside the eat-in kitchen—but she had been glad to get it. A distant cousin of Uncle Jack's, who operated a service station, had recommended this motor court when she had asked about rentals.

"You might get a house or apartment now, but you'd only have to move in a couple of months," he'd warned. "Once the vacation season begins, landlords raise the rents. But a motor court won't be too expensive, even after the first of June."

He must have taken a look at her grungy jeans, tennis shoes, and three-year-old car, and concluded she couldn't afford the fantastic California prices.

He was right.

The small, white stucco house with the flat red roof was so typically Californian, a far cry from the familiar brick, stone, or log homes in North Carolina. But she had an idea she was going to enjoy her privacy. And she was within walking distance of the beach just across the highway.

Uncle Jack's cousin had given her his address and phone number in case she needed him. She was grateful. It made her feel a little more secure, knowing someone to call in an emergency although she'd probably never have to use it. In fact, that was one reason she'd left dear Aunt Sophie. Although her dad's sister had always made Amber feel welcome, she often wondered if Sophie would have married or had a career if she hadn't taken on an orphaned child.

Looking around her now, Amber had to smile. This modest cottage didn't begin to compare with her aunt's two-story Georgian, where Amber had had an entire floor all to herself. But she was satisfied. It felt good to leave the nest and spread her wings. And today, she decided, she'd made a good start.

After tossing a green salad, Amber took the bowl and a glass of iced tea and settled on the couch, only half watching the television set in the corner. She twisted the diamond ring on her finger and felt again an overwhelming sense of guilt. Not only were her own feelings "abnormal," but she'd given the wrong impression to Anton Pasetti.

Still, she was glad she had come. Here, in her own little retreat, she could face the truth about her situation with Ken. Back home, well-meaning friends had smothered her with kindness, assuming she was broken-hearted. Of course, she'd always been fond of Ken. They had attended the same church all their lives. Two years older, he had first sought her out at a singles' Christmas party when she was in her last year of business school and he was a junior at N.C. State. She'd been flattered by the attentions of an "older man."

After that, he'd come home almost every weekend and they'd continued to see each other. The next summer Ken had asked her to marry him.

The proposal had come as a surprise, though in retrospect, she couldn't believe she hadn't seen it coming. They'd been together almost constantly, and their friendship had deepened. But she hadn't been sure how to answer him. Oh, it wasn't that she didn't care for him. He was her best friend.

Initially, it hadn't been his looks that had appealed to her, though he'd been nice-looking enough. Light brown hair. Hazel eyes. Medium build. It was his warm personality, his love for people that had drawn her like a magnet. The compassion that had led him to believe he was being called into the ministry.

Ken was a great guy, all right. The kind of man Amber respected and had always thought she would want to marry. A girl would have been *crazy* to turn him down. So she hadn't. She'd accepted his ring.

In no time at all, the news was out. Aunt Sophie, who had taken Amber in after her parents died, was ecstatic. All her friends were green with envy. So the wedding plans were in motion almost before Amber knew what had happened.

Simultaneously, Ken's uncle, Jack Jackson, had offered her a job with his advertising agency. Ken had wanted to marry right away, but some nagging doubt caused Amber to stall for time. Just because he was that kind of person, he went along with her suggestion that she take the job with his uncle while Ken finished at State. And during his senior year, Amber was promoted to his uncle's personal secretary, then advertising assistant.

In the fall, after graduation, Ken began seminary, and they set the wedding date for the week before Christmas. But as the date neared, Amber grew more apprehensive. Bewildered by her lack of emotion, she prayed often.

She remembered what her pastor had once said about being sure one's plans were in harmony with God's plans. "First of all," he'd said, "don't try to justify something the Bible says is wrong." Well, there was certainly nothing wrong with marrying Ken. "Beyond that, keep your communication lines with God open. Pray, and listen. Listen to the circumstances God puts in your path. Listen to your feelings."

But that was just the problem. Where Ken was concerned, she *had* no feelings. At least, not the kind of feelings she would expect to have for the man she was going to be living with for the rest of her life.

So Amber had listened. She listened to her girlfriends who sometimes dreamed aloud of their wedding night, when they would experience sex with the man they loved. Instead of looking forward to that night, Amber dreaded it. The thought of being intimate with Ken was embarrassing. Oh, she enjoyed his kisses, the warm security she felt in his arms. But anything more than that. . . . Even now, it was difficult to imagine. What was wrong with her? Was she some kind of freak? Or worse? Had her parents' deaths left her unable to respond normally to love?

When her singles' group prayed to be able to resist the

natural physical urges of their bodies, she only mouthed the words. She knew Ken was having difficulty waiting, but for Amber there was no temptation. Maybe that was a blessing. Maybe she'd feel differently after they got married. Now she'd never know.

"I can't go through with it," she'd finally confided to Aunt Sophie just a month before the wedding.

Aunt Sophie had patted her on the arm. "Nonsense! It's just wedding jitters, honey. Everyone has them. They'll pass."

But it wasn't just an attack of nerves. And it hadn't passed.

Amber made up her mind to return Ken's ring. But during the November rains, his car had skidded and crashed on the rain-slick highway on his way home from seminary for Thanksgiving. He had died instantly of a broken neck, so the police report stated. Better that than a broken heart? Amber could only wonder since she'd never had the chance to break their engagement. Now it was her chief consolation. At least he had died believing she loved him as much as he loved her.

Uncle Jack had kindly offered her time off until the first of the year, the weeks designated for her wedding and honeymoon. When she returned in January, she'd asked Uncle Jack what she ought to do with Ken's ring.

Through watery eyes, he had looked down at Amber. "He'd want you to keep it to remember him by." Aunt Sophie had said pretty much the same thing. "True love never ends, honey. Just because he's dead, doesn't mean he isn't still alive in your heart." Of course, Aunt Sophie didn't understand. She'd never married. Instead, she'd dedicated her life to her nursing job and caring for Amber.

Rather than feeling grateful for such generosity, Amber had felt the noose tightening around her emotions. She'd never escape reminders of Ken, never be able to forget her own ambivalence. But removing Ken's ring would seem heartless to these dear people. Not only that, but she had become a kind of martyr in her home town, where daily she heard, "I don't know how you manage to bear up so well, dear. You're truly an inspiration!" or, "We do so admire your courage, Amber."

"I have to get away," Amber had finally told her aunt. She'd bought the second-hand Escort with the insurance money her parents had left her, and because she and Ken had talked about a honeymoon in Florida, she'd decided to travel as far away as possible—in the opposite direction.

It had been Uncle Jack who had given her the idea of coming here to San Diego where he had lived as a boy. "And when you come home," he'd said, "there will be a place for you in the agency."

She smiled at the memory of the kindly man and his earnest offer. But she'd seen the last of North Carolina winters. She'd found a seaside paradise of rocks and cliffs, salt-sea air and swaying palms, and red poinsettias growing wild along the roadside. She had already made one new Christian friend. And she had the faith to believe that there would be other friends and challenges and a new life. Maybe even a new love, a someone who could thaw her frozen heart.

Sorry, Uncle Jack, she thought, *you won't be seeing me any time soon. This is home now.*

three

If they could see me now! Amber frequently mused in the days after her arrival in San Diego. *Small-town girl makes it in the big city!*

The eighth floor of the Pasetti building, with its many offices and shops, was itself much like a small town. On the very first day of the training program, she was given a tour, along with Kate Harvey, who had been hired the same day as Amber. Kate was just out of business school and let Amber know right away that she admired her experience in the working world.

"My dad's in the military and was transferred here three years ago," Kate said in her exuberant way, wrinkling her perky little nose. "I know what it's like to move around a lot and have to make new friends. So from now on, I'm it!"

Amber grinned. "Well, that's an offer I can't refuse." Who could resist Kate? With her big eyes and gamin features, she resembled an eager puppy. And there wasn't a bashful bone in her body. Amber found herself wishing she, too, could be more open, less self-conscious. Yes, Kate Harvey would be good for her.

During the complete beauty makeover, Kate never left Amber's side. She was there to applaud the results of the tips on eye makeup and to mourn with Amber when her long dark hair was trimmed to shoulder length and parted in the middle.

"Shake your head from side to side." Following the stylist's instructions, Amber found that the soft waves that framed her face fell right back into place.

When the makeup artist commented that her skin was like magnolia petals, she blushed. "Ah," he added approvingly, "that's the color we want." He applied the cheek rouge lightly, trying to duplicate what nature had just accomplished.

"Scarlet O'Hara had nothing on you. Hourglass perfect," the wardrobe expert commented on her figure. "With your dark hair and fair skin, you'd be a knockout in vivid colors. Let's try something."

Although she'd never worn the bold color before, when a length of fuschia fabric was held up to her face, the reflection in the mirror didn't lie. She had to agree that the color was flattering.

Later, she couldn't help but laugh, wondering if all this were just a part of the Pasetti plan to build her confidence. "I feel like a model instead of a secretary," she told Kate.

"Isn't it fun? Goes to show that, in my case at least, you *can* make 'a silk purse out of a sow's ear'!" Kate struck a playful pose. "How's *this* for a makeover?"

A touch of green eye shadow gave depth to the dove gray eyes, and the short cap of light brown curls suited Kate's outgoing personality. "I don't mind being a secretary here," she told Amber. "Even that position is glamorous."

There was thorough training in general office procedures, as well. Both Lynn and one of Charis's most experienced assistants briefed Amber and Kate, giving them on-the-job assignments: handling phone calls, greeting clients, and learning the company computer system. The time flew.

Over the weekend, Amber and Kate found another

mutual interest—shopping. On Sunday, they attended a little church near Amber's cottage and went out for lunch together afterward. In the afternoon, Amber called Aunt Sophie, who was thrilled with Amber's new job and the fact that she had made friends, especially "that fine Christian woman at work," her aunt said. "My prayers are being answered, honey!"

When Amber mentioned Uncle Jack, she was surprised to hear that Aunt Sophie was cooking supper for him and that he'd be arriving "any time now."

"Oh, I'm so glad you're having company in, Aunt Sophie. Jack Jackson is such a nice man."

There was a prickle of curiosity along with the little stab of guilt. Her aunt had never complained about missing out on a personal social life because of her care of Amber. But if anyone deserved a "nice man"—someone to take care of *her* for a change—it was Sophie. "Have fun, you two!" Amber said, and smiled as she replaced the receiver.

❧

Three weeks slipped by, and at the end of the day on Friday, Charis called Amber into her office. Her smile was as warm and charming as ever. "We've had a little. . . change of plans."

Wondering about the "we," Amber looked at her expectantly.

"Mr. Pasetti has decided he wants you as his personal secretary."

Amber froze in her seat.

"Do you have some problem with that arrangement?"

"Oh, don't think I'm ungrateful," Amber roused herself enough to say. "I just thought. . .that is, I'd hoped to work for *you*."

"What a nice compliment. And I can't say I'm not disappointed that we won't be working together more closely," Charis said kindly. "But we must take ability and experience into consideration as well as personality type. Kate is a dear, but I'm afraid her effervescence might annoy some of our clients. Also, you must know she finds Anton absolutely fascinating." She laughed softly. "It was a blow to his ego to learn that *you don't.*"

"Why would he think a thing like that?" Amber was almost amused. As far as she was concerned, everyone in this new world of high fashion was fascinating.

Charis gave her an appraising glance. "I feel I can trust you, Amber, though I wouldn't confide in just anyone. The day he hired you, Anton felt you didn't particularly like him. And I must admit, I *have* noticed. . .a certain reserve when you're around him.

"Oh, not that you're anything but unfailingly courteous and respectful. . .just a little distant. None of that hero worship he's come to expect in a new employee."

Amber stared down at her manicured nails and wondered how to respond. It was true that she respected Anton Pasetti for his business acumen, but she certainly didn't idolize him just because he happened to run a worldwide empire. Her aunt, maybe, for taking her in and being a mother to her. Or someone like Ken, who had planned to spend his life in the ministry, telling others about Jesus. But this cocky, self-important man? No. It wasn't hero worship she felt.

"Of course I understand," Charis continued, following Amber's gaze to the engagement ring on her finger. "Right now, you probably feel as if you could never be interested in any man again. But that could change. . .after you've had a little more time to heal. There are some fine young men in San Diego." Amber couldn't bear to look into the woman's face, so she said nothing and kept her head bowed. "I want you to know that my prayer group is remembering you."

Amber dropped her head even lower, hoping her hair would conceal any expression of dismay. "Thank you," she mumbled, feeling like a moth caught in a spider web. Was there no way out of this? She must clear up the misunderstanding about the ring. But now didn't seem to be the time. When she glanced up, she didn't miss the look of sympathy in Charis's eyes. "I. . .hope Mr. Pasetti didn't think I was being rude."

"No problem, dear. Anton is completely convinced you'll be the efficient, detached secretary he needs. And—I hope you don't mind—I also told him that you're a Christian." Surprised, Amber lifted a brow. "Oh, don't worry. He was very pleased to hear it. Said dedicated Christians make the best employees."

"What about Mr. Pasetti's beliefs?" Amber couldn't help asking. "Is *he* a Christian?"

"Not that I know of," Charis replied somewhat wistfully. "Quite a few of my friends in the business are in the same boat. It's almost impossible to persuade people they need the Lord when they have so much of this world's goods." The corner of her mouth quirked in a wry smile. "I know. I've been there."

Amber nodded. Her association with the rich and famous was limited, but she had already discovered that in these new surroundings, her faith was not always understood. At least Kate was willing to discuss it. But most of the others seemed to feel that choice of lifestyle, including what one believed about God, was a personal matter. Which, to Amber, translated: "None of your business!" A couple of people had even laughed it off. "Oh, you're from the South, aren't you? What's it called. . .the Bible Belt?"

How could she make them understand that her faith was not something to be endured, but was the most important part of her life?

Judging from what Charis said, Anton Pasetti, too, probably considered her faith quaint but harmless. She forced a smile. "I'll do my best for Mr. Pasetti."

"Good girl. I knew I could count on you. Anton and I both feel you can handle the additional responsibilities rather than being just another secretary in the pool." Her blue eyes danced. "Not to mention that the salary is better."

Charis extended her hand, and Amber noticed, as she had on the first day they met, that the older woman was wearing several large rings on her fingers, including a wedding band. "Just give it a try. . .and after a few weeks, if you don't feel it's the right spot for you, we'll see what we can do."

Amber was touched. The woman was a walking example of the Pasetti ideal, always charming and tactful, always putting the other person at ease. It was the kind of assurance Amber needed on the last day of training; on Monday, she would begin working directly with Anton Pasetti.

Although she had seen him only from a distance during the past few weeks, she had not failed to notice him when he dropped by to observe some aspect of the training sessions. Always, she had had the feeling he had been watching her, evaluating her, and weighing her assets. There was some satisfaction in knowing she had met some kind of criteria.

But at the back of her mind, there was the niggling sense that there would be times in the weeks and months ahead when she would wish she had never met the man!

four

On Monday morning a tall, crystal vase of deep red roses was waiting on the desk when Amber walked into the reception room of the Pasetti Modeling Agency.

"Somebody's birthday?" she asked Lynn as she parked her purse in the desk drawer.

"They're for *you.*"

"For *me?*" Amber eyed her skeptically, then slipped the small card from the envelope attached and read it out loud. "Welcome, Amber! Anton Pasetti."

Contrary to her weeks of training in poise and self-control, she brought her hand to her mouth in an involuntary gesture of surprise. "Is this. . .standard operating procedure?"

Lynn shrugged. "I wouldn't know. Anton's *mother* hired me five years ago." At Amber's puzzled expression, she laughed. "Don't try to analyze it. Just enjoy."

Amber was bending over to inhale the fragrance of one perfect bud when she heard movement behind her.

"Good morning, Anton," Lynn greeted him, then busied herself at the file cabinet.

Lynn called him by his first name? Amber knew an employee could take such liberties only if the employer had invited it, or if there were no clients around to overhear. But what was she expected to do? She'd better play it safe.

Turning to glance over her shoulder, she was temporarily distracted by the fact that he was so much taller than she remembered. "Good morning, Anton," she blurted before she corrected herself in a professional, three-week-trained tone, "Uh. . .I mean, good morning, Mr. Pasetti. And thank you for the roses. They're very beautiful."

He returned the greeting, adding softly, "And so are you, Amber."

Her intake of breath was audible as she lost her composure for the second time in as many minutes.

His manner changed abruptly. "Oh, don't take it personally. Beauty is our business here. . .remember? Our models, secretaries, even the waitresses in the cafeteria are expected to be beautiful."

He was still talking as he walked over to the coffee urn and poured himself a cup of coffee. "My mother, who founded this agency on the philosophy that every woman is innately beautiful, believed that with the right clothes, the proper hair style, and careful makeup, even the most homely can be attractive."

Why did he have to add a disclaimer to what had seemed like a simple compliment? Flustered, Amber tried to cover her self-consciousness. "Well, she must have been right, because I certainly haven't seen anyone around *here* who is unattractive."

He peered at her over the rim of his cup, one dark brow lifted.

Realizing how he must be interpreting her casual comment, she wondered if she had already committed the unpardonable sin by Pasetti standards. One of two things might be grounds for dismissal: developing ambitions to be a model . . .or developing designs on the boss!

Almost immediately she felt a stiffening of resolve. She didn't care the first thing about being a model. Besides, she had always believed that true beauty was far more than mere outward appearance. Pasetti training addressed part of it, emphasizing courtesy and consideration for others. But there was another kind of inner beauty Amber knew and that was a humility and selflessness that came only from a heart transformed by God.

As for Anton Pasetti, she had to admit that his "outward appearance" was enough to make any woman do a double take. For example, this morning he was dressed casually in dark pants and a creamy white silk shirt, open at the neck, that emphasized his tan. But he was her *boss* and at least ten years older than she. More than that, they were from two different worlds and—*What am I thinking?* she groaned inwardly.

Muttering something about getting a cup of coffee, she moved past him and toward the urn. She began to relax only when she heard his office door open and close behind him. *Well, Amber, you've managed to get off to a fine start!* she berated herself. *That man and I just don't speak the same language!* But she suspected that their dismal inability to communicate had little to do with her southern accent.

Lynn closed the file drawer with a snap, breaking Amber's reverie. "Come on. I'll show you around. We'll start with the storage closet since you'll be needing some supplies before long." She led the way to a door on the opposite side of the room, opened it, and motioned Amber inside.

Amber took note of the well-stocked shelves. From floor to ceiling, all kinds of office supplies were arranged in neat stacks—from boxes of computer disks and fax paper to paper clips. While they were safely out of ear-shot, she ventured a question. "What's it like to work for Mr. Pasetti?" she began, keeping her tone light. "I mean, what kind of person is he?"

"He's really a fine man," Lynn replied after a thoughtful pause. "And incidentally, he wasn't flirting with you just now. No offense, but why should he? He has the most beautiful women in the world literally falling at his feet."

Amber felt justifiably reprimanded. According to Charis, Anton Pasetti needed a sensible secretary, not one who would distract him from his work. Well, Amber was noth-ing if not sensible. And she hadn't the slightest intention of becoming another name on his list of ardent admirers.

They left the storage room and Lynn closed the door, mov-ing to a pile of mail on the desk. She thumbed through as she continued, "He's pretty demanding, and sometimes you'll wonder if you can possibly get everything done. But that's the kind of business we're in. Sometimes things can't wait until morning, so there's some overtime that goes with the territory. Oh, don't worry," she assured, spotting Amber's look of distress, "Anton is all business at times like that.

"And he's fair. He won't expect you to pull off the impossible all by yourself." Lynn gestured toward a smaller desk. "That's for the days when you're swamped and need to call in a backup. All you have to do is check with Charis, and she'll send someone over. It's all going to work out."

❧

During the week, Lynn briefed Amber on her duties, watch-ing over her shoulder as she got the hang of it. By the middle of the week, Amber was on her own, fielding questions on the phone, drafting contracts for models, and sorting Mr. Pasetti's personal mail. And by the end of the week, she had even learned to tell when he was too busy or preoccupied to pour his own coffee, and began to take it to him on a tray, along with the mail and business section of the *Wall Street Journal*.

On those mornings he never looked up from his desk, but barely acknowledged her presence with a nod or a wave of his hand. Even when he called her in to use her laptop to take down a a business letter, he dictated with a brisk authority that did not invite response. On Thursday evening, one contract required two hours of overtime, but he made no apology. "We'll stay until this is finished," he said. And when the final draft was delivered to his desk for his signature, there was not a word of thanks.

At the end of the day on Friday, just after Lynn had packed up her things and left for the last time, and Amber was getting ready to lock up, a gorgeous redhead burst into the office, demanding to see "Anton." She practically purred his name, Amber thought with a trace of annoyance.

Amber had seen Gina around the building a few times and knew she was the model being considered for a shampoo commercial for television, which accounted for one of the reasons they had been so busy all week. Well, they couldn't miss with Gina, Amber had to admit, eyeing the young woman's luxuriant mane of fiery red hair.

Amber pressed the buzzer, but Mr. Pasetti was already on his way out of his office door. Spotting Gina standing near Amber's desk, he beamed, white teeth flashing in his tanned face. And with little more than a perfunctory, "Good night," they left without a backward glance. Was this some unscheduled business appointment? Amber shrugged. Since she hadn't been invited along to take notes, she supposed it must be more personal than professional. But it was no business of hers.

She glanced at the roses. They looked about as wilted as she felt. At the first of the week, she had put an aspirin in the water to keep the buds from opening too soon. But now she could see that the flowers couldn't possibly last until Monday. Might as well get rid of them. With a sigh, she tossed them into the trash can.

Suddenly she wished she could be working instead of facing what promised to be a lonely weekend. Kate was going away with her parents. The singles at church usually had their own weekend projects lined up. She supposed she could clean the cottage, but with only one occupant—a neatnik at that—it wasn't really dirty. Maybe she could go shopping for accessories to go with some of her new outfits. But why bother? She certainly didn't have any dates lined up. She'd met a few guys, but after noticing the diamond on her finger, they'd kept their distance.

On a whim, she tugged at the ring, but it wouldn't come off. Shrugging aside a twinge of guilt, she locked up and left the office.

ঌ

Accustomed to business hours during the workweek, Amber awoke early the next morning. She stretched, feeling the pull of little-used muscles. There had been no time for physical fitness with a new job and settling into her new living quarters. Better do something about that.

In the kitchen she spread a bagel with low-fat cream cheese, then nibbled while she spooned coffee into the pot. After her light breakfast, she threw on a pair of shorts

and a tank top and sprinted across the highway to the beach.
By the time she reached the shore, she was wide awake.

The sun, rising behind her, slanted its rays across the tur-
quoise water, more calm than she had ever seen it. No swells.
No waves. Nothing to disturb the glassy surface, it was
much like a lake. She felt the bittersweet tug of nostalgic
memories of family vacations beside a lake in North Carolina. She had always loved going there—until her parents
had been drowned in a boating accident and she had moved
in with Aunt Sophie. Neither Amber nor her aunt had returned to the lake since. Still, the ocean was different.

A breeze blew up, riffling the water and sending gentle
waves washing up on the beach. Amber began to run. She
jogged steadily until she came to a rocky section of shoreline.
When she felt the pebbles underfoot, she slowed to catch
her breath, panting in the fresh sea air. With the blood singing
in her veins, she felt a sense of exhilaration like nothing she
had felt since she and Ken had played tennis together.

Looking back down the beach, she saw that her footprints, chased by the sea, had already disappeared. There
was nothing to indicate from which direction she had come
. . .or where she was going. She had run halfway across
the country, it seemed, not *toward* anything in particular,
but *away* from something. Now she must allow the past,
like her footprints in the sand, to be washed from her mind.

At that moment, Ken's diamond glinted in the sunlight.
Amber glanced at her hand, then out over the ocean. Bury-
ing her toes in the warm sand, she squared her shoulders.
It was time. Today she would take off the ring and put it
away. Today it would be over.

She watched the sun skidding into a hazy blue sky and,
with a little ache in her heart, she breathed, "Good-bye, Ken."

five

It was Gina who first noticed the missing diamond. "No ring?" she asked Amber when she breezed in unexpectedly on Tuesday. Her tone was more condescending than concerned. "Well, I'm sure there's another nice young man out there somewhere. Anton's in, I suppose?"

Amber lifted her hand to press the intercom button. "I'll let him know you're here."

Gina shot her an exasperated look. "Oh, that's not necessary. He'll see me."

"I'm only following Mr. Pasetti's orders. I'm to announce anyone—"

"But I'm not just *any*one, honey." Gina tossed her glorious hair and swept past Amber and into Anton's office.

Amber felt her face flame with hot anger. But later, when her boss said nothing about his unexpected visitor, Amber could only assume that Gina was right: she was not just "anyone." After that, the redhead spared few words for Amber, but barged into the executive office whenever she pleased.

❧

In the following month the agency buzzed with activity. Mr. Pasetti was either preparing for or conducting one business meeting after another. There were endless luncheons and dinners and board meetings. For the most part, Amber handled the job without difficulty, though she often called Lynn for advice and Charis for extra help.

One situation Amber hadn't counted on was the stream of models coming in to see Anton. Some came at his request, to discuss the details of an upcoming contract. These he treated with cool courtesy. Others came in, weepy and red-eyed, disappointed over some job they'd failed to snag. These he referred to Charis.

"I've had enough trouble with women hounding me," he told Amber one morning in a rare moment of openness, "without letting them cry on my shoulder when a deal goes sour."

They are broad, she was thinking, inadvertently glancing at his very masculine, very impressive set of shoulders. Well, he could be assured she wouldn't be blubbering all over those manly shoulders! However, with his peering at her over the rim of his coffee cup, a trace of blue glinting in his dark eyes, she felt an uncomfortable warmth creeping through her body, all the way to her hairline.

"What a becoming shade of pink," he observed conversationally. "Too bad our makeup department can't bottle that glow."

Pleading a pile of work on her desk, Amber fled just before the flood of color returned. Just the week before, she had given his roses an aspirin to retard their opening. Right now she considered popping one in her own mouth, then scolded herself under her breath, "Stop it right now, Amber! That's unprofessional behavior. So what if this is the first time the boss has noticed that you're not a machine!"

❧

By the end of May, the pace at the office had slowed long

enough for the executives to catch their breath. Amber was using her laptop in Mr. Pasetti's office when she caught him staring at her left hand. Was this the first time he had noticed the missing ring?

He broke his stare, stood, and turned toward the windows, flexing his shoulders to work out the kinks. Amber had the feeling he'd rather be elsewhere, probably somewhere with Gina. He had finished his dictation, so she rose to leave.

He must have heard her movement, for he turned and faced her. "Say, Amber, how are the RSVPs coming along for the picnic?"

Supervising the publicity and recording the reservations for the company's annual get-together had occupied a great deal of Amber's time lately, but it wasn't high on her list of personal priorities. Even though everyone from Charis Lamarr to the custodian had been invited, she wasn't even sure she wanted to go. It had been a long time, a very long time, since she'd attended a party. That last time had been with Ken. "We've heard from most of them."

"I assume you're planning to be there." The inflection of his voice left no room for speculation.

"I. . .haven't decided yet."

He appeared shocked. "No one ever refuses an invitation to a Pasetti picnic," was he only pretending to be stern? "unless it's a dire emergency. We've even had employees come with broken legs."

At the absurd idea, Amber had to laugh along with him, then looked away from his disconcerting gaze. This relaxed, more congenial Anton Pasetti only confused her.

"You have other plans?" he pursued. "A world cruise, perhaps?"

"Oh, nothing so glamorous." She was trying desperately to keep the conversation light. "I'm afraid my boss wouldn't give me that much time off."

"Right you are!" Anton was emphatic. "Good secretaries are hard to find. And your boss is too smart to let her get away." Abruptly the tone of his voice shifted slightly. "You still don't like me, though, do you, Amber?"

She eyed him quizzically, but he had turned again to look out the window. "I realize that in the workplace it's best to keep things on an impersonal basis. And to be honest, it's something of a relief to know that you'll not be pestering me for a modeling contract. I think every one of Charis's secretaries has cornered me at one time or another—in the elevator, in the coffee shop, and even in the parking lot."

Amber allowed a fleeting smile. It was a well-known fact and the topic of a lot of office gossip.

His voice mellowed as he faced her again. "So I appreciate your sensible approach to our working relationship. However, let me make myself clear. Your. . .aloofness doesn't have to extend past closing time."

His eyes met hers briefly, but she couldn't make out the expression in them. In fact, she wondered what he was getting at, although she wasn't about to ask.

After an awkward pause, his voice once again took on a more businesslike tone. "I thought you understood that your services might be required after hours."

"Of course. Lynn told me. And during our training, Charis. . .Mrs. Lamarr instructed all of us about office hours." She would *not* let his arrogance ruffle her. "I don't mind working overtime once in a while. But. . .I don't understand what that has to do—"

"Don't you know by now, *Miss* Jennings," his exaggerated patience making her feel like a school dropout, "that a great deal of business is conducted during social events?"

"You mean. . .the picnic?"

Looking smug, he silenced her with an uplifted hand. "Exactly. I had hoped you might be available. Your presence would be. . .helpful. But if you have more important things to do, by all means do them." She could only stare. "I'll just get someone else to help with the cleanup afterward. . . as Lynn did last year."

He moved his chair nearer the desk and began to sort through some papers. She felt dismissed.

Thinking it over, she supposed this request wasn't so different from his orders to "Bring the Burman file, Amber. We have to see him over lunch," or "Get a replacement for your desk. I'll need you to take notes at a called board meeting this afternoon." Looking at it that way, the picnic was just part of her job. "If you need me, Mr. Pasetti, of course I'll be there."

With only a nod to acknowledge that he'd heard her, Amber returned to her desk, her mind in high gear. She'd have to take something other than casual clothes, in case of another called meeting of the board or something equally significant. At least she'd learned that a Pasetti employee must be prepared for anything. Lynn might have some tips, too.

At home, Amber picked up the phone and called her. "What kind of cleanup does Mr. Pasetti expect after the picnic? I would have thought the caterers would arrange for that. But he seemed to want me to help. Said you'd done it last year."

"He didn't ask me, Amber. I volunteered. But I must

have done *some* terrific job for him to remember." Lynn
went on to explain that Anton had plenty of hired help for his
elaborate bashes. "But there are usually a few stray items
the others miss. You know what a perfectionist Anton is.
Or. . . ," there was a long pause, "maybe he just wants to
enjoy your company after everyone else has left."

"Ha! I doubt that!" Amber snorted. "What he wants is
a cleaning lady!"

But Lynn's parting words lingered long after they had
hung up. Enjoy her company? Ridiculous! Anton Pasetti
was surrounded by the most beautiful women in the world.
Lynn herself had reminded her earlier. Why would he
want to spend time with *her?* Maybe he was just trying
to prove a point. The man's ego probably couldn't toler-
ate the thought that at least one woman wasn't wild about
him! Well, she had no desire to fall for a guy who no
doubt discarded women like other men cast off an old pair
of shoes.

As the date of the picnic neared, Amber asked Kate to
ride to the affair with her. Her friend even agreed to help
with the cleanup, so they could leave together afterward.
With Kate around, there would be no chance of an awkward confrontation with Anton Pasetti. Just what she
wanted, right?

ঞ

The noon sun, dead overhead, blazed mercilessly in a hot
sky, striking sparks, it seemed, from the frothing ocean.
Kate and Amber, in the Escort, followed a teal green Sub-
urban packed with Charis's employees. The road curved
along the coastline, climbing gently but persistently into
the hills.

At last the caravan turned onto a brick driveway flanked

by tall, carefully trimmed hedges. Farther up the incline could be seen the tops of swaying palms. And perched atop the cliff, a gleaming white structure that reminded Amber of something from a tourist brochure.

"There's even a bell tower!" Kate exclaimed, bouncing out of the car.

Even with her sunglasses, Amber had to shade her eyes against the bright sunlight to see an enormous tower suspended from the top of the two-tiered structure.

"The architecture of the house is patterned after the old Spanish missions," explained Donna, one of the secretaries, as she got out of Charis's van. "But just wait till you see the back!"

Amber gestured for the others to lead the way. Their sandals flapped against the terra cotta tiles as they walked across the front of the house, under an arcade supported by tall, slender columns. Between each pair of columns was an arch, and beneath each arch, a massive container of tropical flowers.

They turned a corner to another arcade that extended all the way to the back of the house, stopping at a pair of black wrought-iron gates. Donna unfastened them, swung the grillwork open, and, with a sweep of her hand, announced, "Welcome to Paradise!"

Mouth agape, Amber stepped through the gates and into another world. At the center of the tiled patio was a fountain, guarded by two carved stone lions. Sparkling water spewed high into the air, then fell back to the base again in graceful arcs. A low wall encircled the patio. Several of the guests who had arrived earlier had already found seats there and were chatting in congenial groups.

Beyond the patio Amber could see the formal gardens:

sculptured shrubbery, an occasional tree for shade, and a riot of flowers.

"You two going swimming?" Donna spoke up, pointing to the pool and cabana beyond the gardens.

"Count me in!" Kate waved a tote bag packed with her swimming gear.

"You go ahead," Amber told her. "I'd like to walk around for a while first."

Kate and Donna hurried off, and Amber made her way over to the fountain to catch some of the cooling spray. The sun was beating down, and she welcomed the breeze drifting through the courtyard, stirring the wisps at the back of her neck. Good thing she had taken time to pull her hair into a ponytail.

Looking around, she was relieved to see that most of the other women were dressed as casually as she, in shorts and scoop-necked shirts. Apparently the Pasetti look could bend if the occasion called for it. Only a couple of models had chosen sundresses, but they were lounging in the coolest part of the patio, under the arcade.

"Drink, miss?"

Amber turned to find a middle-aged woman in a crisp white uniform, holding a tray of iced beverages.

"Oh, thank you." Amber selected a tall glass of clear liquid, garnished with a sprig of mint.

Other uniformed employees—the men in white jackets with gold buttons and black pants—circulated among the guests, serving hors d'oeuvres—plump pink shrimp nested on lush beds of lettuce, dainty finger sandwiches, hot canapés.

So this was the famous Pasetti picnic! It was like no other Amber had ever attended. No mounds of golden fried chicken. No ants. No juicy watermelon eaten down to the rind, with a seed-spitting contest afterward.

Amber tentatively brought the liquid to her lips. The drink was wonderfully refreshing—some kind of iced concoction of whipped fruit—and, to her surprise, *no alcohol.* Anton Pasetti must share at least some of her convictions, she thought. Or maybe he was only protecting his models' health and welfare.

"Hi, Amber." A familiar male voice called from behind her, and she turned to see Ron Jordan, a male model from the agency, with his friend Jim Meyers, who worked in advertising.

"Ready for a swim?" Ron flashed a million-watt smile. He often did shoots featuring those perfect white teeth—toothpaste ads, tanning salons, that kind of thing.

"I don't think Mr. Pasetti would approve," she teased, glancing at the fountain.

Ron chuckled. "Not here! Jim tells me there's a pool. Come on down."

Keeping up with the long strides of the two men, Amber had little time to appreciate the gardens and promised herself she'd revisit them before the day ended.

Since she hadn't come prepared to swim, she waited at a table shaded by a wide umbrella while they changed in the cabana. At one end of the Olympic-sized pool were several diving boards, set at varying heights. Following the gaze of the bystanders, she turned to see a figure poised on the high dive.

Anton Pasetti did not look anything like a businessman today. His bronzed body gleamed in the sun, and something silver glinted at his neck. Typical of his style, his dive was executed with perfect skill and grace.

When he broke the water and pulled himself from the pool

in a single fluid motion, she gasped. She had known his shoulders were broad, but had not guessed at his lean, muscular physique. *He must work out in a gym or health club,* Amber suspected. *That body takes work.*

She looked on as he waved to a youngster—an employee's child probably—splashing nearby. Midway down the side of the pool, a lifeguard sat erect, watching.

Kate called to Amber from the shallow end, and she called back. When Anton spotted her, he stood and made his way over to her table, his dripping form towering above her. Her eyes swept upward, and a flash of sunlight caught the silver chain that rested above the patch of dark hair, wet and curled, on his chest. She dropped her gaze in embarrassment.

"Hadn't you planned to swim, Amber?"

"Oh, I'd rather watch," she said quickly, grateful for the children's antics in the pool that gave her an excuse to look away. "Everything here is so. . .beautiful," she finished feebly.

She risked a glance. He was wiping away a drop of water that was sliding down his nose from the lock of hair plastered over his forehead. It was the first time she had ever seen a single hair out of place; it gave him a young, boyish look, despite the silver at his temples.

"You *do* swim?"

She nodded, playing with the stem of her glass. "Believe it or not, I used to be pretty athletic. Spent many a summer at a lake in my younger days. . .Mr. Pasetti." She still didn't feel comfortable calling him by his first name, not even at the company picnic.

He laughed, his teeth white against the darkening tan of his face. "Well, you're not quite ready for a retirement home, so far as I can tell, Miss Jennings." His bold gaze swept her from head to toe. "Just what *do* you enjoy doing for recreation. . .now that you're an old lady?"

Now he was making fun of her. She thrust out her chin. "Tennis is my sport."

"Oh?" He lifted a water-slick brow. "You'll have to schedule a game with Charis's husband. He's practically a pro."

She shook her head. "Then I'd be no match for him. I'm just an amateur." Hoping to change the subject, she scanned the surroundings—the tiled poolside, fringed with waving palms, the manicured lawn sloping down to the terrace. "You have a lovely place here, Mr. Pasetti."

There was a twinkle of amusement in his eyes. "Then remind me to give you a guided tour of the house. . .later." With a little salute, he strolled away, speaking to other guests on his way back to the diving board.

The perfect gentleman, Amber thought, *that's all it is. He's charming and polite to everyone.*

She took the last sip from the glass, set it on the table, and started in the direction of the house.

"Amber." Hearing her name, she saw Charis Lamarr, impeccable in an ice blue linen pants suit, standing in the arcade behind the patio. A tall, lean man, who appeared to be in his sixties, was at her side. His deep tan contrasted with a shock of white hair. "Come meet my Leonard," Charis called gaily.

"Ah. . .another beautiful model." Leonard Lamarr took her hand and kissed it in the continental manner.

Amber smiled at the twinkle in his eyes. "Afraid not. I'm just a secretary."

"She could easily be a model, though," Charis agreed,

walking over to find a seat in the shade. Leonard brought another chair for Amber. "But Anton has hired her as his assistant. I told you about her, Len."

"Not quite *everything,* my dear."

With a musical laugh, Charis laid her hand over her husband's sun-browned one. Amber felt a bit uneasy under Leonard Lamarr's close scrutiny. Why was he studying her like that?

Seeing Amber's puzzled look, Charis explained. "Len has a line of cosmetics, specializing in eye makeup. Since he often uses our models in his advertisements, it's only natural that he views every woman he meets as a possibility."

"Oh, I'm not the one for your line, Mr. Lamarr, though I'm flattered."

"I realize I'm an old codger, Amber, but I'd consider it a favor if you'd just call me Len."

"All right. . .Len." Amber settled back against the cushions, feeling more at ease with this friendly couple than she had felt all day. Despite their good looks and prestigious positions, they might be the grandparents she'd never known.

They chatted companionably. Amber learned that it was Anton's mother who had improved the property, styling the house after the Spanish missions so prevalent in southern California, adding wings, and planning the exquisite gardens.

"It's truly magnificent," Amber breathed, still stunned by the beauty around her.

"Anton's mother was lovely, inside and out," Charis said with a trace of sadness. "We all miss her so much, particularly Anton, of course."

"Speaking of the devil. . . ," Len gestured toward the garden.

"Len!" Charis reprimanded with a helpless shake of her head. "We love that boy as if he were our own," she confided to Amber.

Her gaze following Len's gesture, Amber spotted her handsome boss. From out of nowhere, as if she had been awaiting the moment to make her entrance, Gina appeared at his side. She was wearing a copper-colored bikini that emphasized her lush curves and echoed her glorious hair, which was partially covered by a floppy, wide-brimmed hat. Her pale skin—a translucent ivory—looked as if it had never been touched by the sun and, if it were, it would freckle.

Anton was still in his wet swim trunks, but the rest of him was dry, including his tousled hair, which now curled over his forehead. Once again Amber was reminded of a naughty little boy, whose eager zest for life, like the unruly curls, could not be contained.

Gina, like some tawny predator, moved in to stake her claim, touching the silver chain at his throat and laughing up into his face. Chuckling at something she had said, Anton looked fondly down at her, his hands grasping the ends of a towel slung around his neck. *They're a stunning couple,* Amber thought with just a touch of envy. *I wonder if anyone will ever look at me like that.*

She turned her head to find Len's gaze fixed on her. She squirmed, embarrassed to be caught like a kid outside a candy store. Well, she wouldn't be so transparent again. She was about to strike up a conversation with Charis when Anton came striding toward them, his business with Gina apparently at an end.

"You may have yourself a challenge here, Len," Anton said as he joined them. "Amber tells me that tennis is her game."

"Oh, I'm no match for a star," she corrected.

"Any starring role for me was over many moons ago, my dear," Len said, then chuckled. "Still, I'd like to take you up on that challenge one of these days. But at the moment, Anton, it's her *eyes* I'm interested in. I'm sure you've noticed."

Amber felt herself on the hot seat again as all three heads swiveled in her direction. "My eyes? They're just an ordinary mouse brown. You're teasing me, Len."

"Len?" Anton seemed surprised. "Now how do you rate a relationship with my secretary on a first-name basis? I'd venture to say you two have never met before today."

Leonard winked. "Always did have a way with beautiful women."

Anton flicked his towel lightly at the older man in a gesture of affection, Amber suspected. Lulled by their easy camaraderie and the warmth of the day, she relaxed even more. But when the Lamarrs and Anton fell into conversation about the upkeep of the grounds, as if it were home to all of them, she began to feel like an intruder.

"There's Kate," she said, seizing an opportunity to leave. "We promised to spend some time together, since we're the newest additions to the agency."

"*The family* would be a more apt description," Len corrected. "And most welcome additions, I'm sure."

Amber turned a grateful smile on this man who had set her so at ease from the beginning, and she wondered at the kindred spirit between them. He must be a Christian, like Charis. She'd noticed that with most people who shared the same faith in God, there seemed to be an instantaneous bond, just as there was an invisible wall separating her from those who did not—like Anton Pasetti.

The older couple rose to leave. "See you later, you two," Charis called with a waggle of her fingers.

Amber jumped to her feet. No way did she want to be alone with her enigmatic boss. Besides, he was probably just as ready to be rid of her. She managed to excuse herself and walk away without tripping over the loose tile at the edge of the patio.

On her way to catch up with Kate, Amber thought of Len's remark about family. That concept seemed to be Anton Pasetti's goal for the agency. If it really was a family, then Anton was the head. Everyone *did* look up to him. But why shouldn't they? Of course they admired him; he was a successful businessman, the man who signed their paycheck. Still, today she had seen a different side to Anton Pasetti, a more human side, a genuine caring for others. It reminded her of the day he'd asked her to find out what Lynn might need for her new baby and had then, on his own, arranged for a baby nurse for the first two weeks.

It would be nice to be part of a family again, she mused. As a child, she had assumed her parents would always be around loving her, protecting her. Later, she had believed Ken was her safe harbor. But of course, it was out of the question to lean on Anton Pasetti. She had decided long ago never to allow herself to care deeply about a man who was not a Christian.

Now, remembering his masculine appeal, his charm and consideration, she tried to shut out an errant thought that a man who cared about older people and babies must not be all bad!

six

Brushing away a loose strand of hair straggling from her ponytail, Amber walked over to the fountain where Kate was standing with Jim and Ron. The three had changed back into their casual clothes, their hair still wet from their shower. "Have a good swim?"

"Just enough to work up a huge appetite!" Ron replied with a dazzling smile.

Jim glanced at his watch. "You'll have to hang on for twenty more minutes, pal. When Anton Pasetti says dinner will be served at six o'clock, that's exactly what he means."

"No problem," Kate said with a shrug. "We can walk around the gardens until then."

When they returned, servants had opened the french doors and were inviting the guests to come in.

"This is not exactly the way I'd pictured the picnic," Amber whispered to Kate. "I expected to eat off a tablecloth spread on the ground."

Kate wrinkled her turned-up nose. "I can't imagine an ant daring to crash *this* party!" she said with a giggle.

From the foyer, the guests entered a spacious room with dark tile and paneling. Long tables were set along the walls; behind them stood waiters in tall white hats, serving elegant food onto china plates. It was a veritable feast, with every imaginable delicacy—thin slices of roast beef and pork, fajitas, tacos, and quesadillas to offer the flavor of the Southwest, several rich casseroles, and a cornucopia of fruit, topped with a plumed pineapple and cascading from the center of the table. Another smaller table contained trays filled with pastries and a Mexican flan.

With their plates filled to overflowing, the guests found their way back outside through another pair of french doors and seated themselves at one of several tables or on the low wall encircling the courtyard. The entertainment began when most of the guests had put their plates aside and sat sipping their beverages. Strolling guitarists in Mexican costumes, complete with sombreros, paraded around the patio, serenading them.

At the close of one sprightly number, the musicians took seats on the edge of the fountain and began strumming a love song. A man with jet black hair and a white shirt tucked into his black breeches and a woman in a long, ruffled red dress, made a dramatic appearance from opposite sides of the courtyard. While the man stood rigid, arms folded over his chest, the woman began to dance to the song, sung alternately in Spanish and English.

Amber was intrigued. The woman tossed her flowing raven hair, tapping her feet with staccato steps to the music, slowly at first, then with increasing speed. The tall lover stood aloof while she whirled around him, inviting him to join her with a look. Finally he could remain indifferent to her wiles no longer and entered into the dance, expressing in every movement his love for the beautiful señorita.

The dance stirred Amber deeply, at some level she dared not acknowledge. When it was finished, she applauded along with the others, then let out a long sigh. It was only a dance, she reminded herself. The couple were not in love; they were performers, paid by Pasetti money.

And, as many of the guests began to drift away, Amber recalled why she was here in the first place. Anton Pasetti had summoned her to clean up after the picnic. She'd better get busy.

"I'm going to get my change of clothes and makeup kit from the car," Amber told Kate, feeling a strange letdown. "I may have to take notes for a meeting. If you'll stick around, we'll clean up when I get back."

"Amber?" Kate could not conceal her excitement. "Would you mind terribly if Jim took me home?" Her eyes were pleading.

Amber could never refuse her friend. "Of course not. That's great. You two go ahead, and I'll see you Monday."

"But you asked me to help pick up, and I'm feeling really guilty about this."

"There won't be that much to do," Amber assured her. "Unless Mr. Pasetti does have a meeting scheduled, I'll be out of here in no time. Now, scoot!"

"Well, I think Ron is going to ask to take *you* home," Kate added with a sly grin.

That was no surprise. Amber had already figured it was coming. But she had work to do first. She hurried to the car, retrieved her things, and went back to the house to find a guest room. Not quite sure what the evening would bring, she had packed a full skirt and multicolored blouse appropriate to the surroundings. She slipped on a pair of strappy sandals and gold dangling loops in her ears, then repaired her makeup and brushed out her ponytail until her hair hung softly around her shoulders. Mr. Pasetti should have given her a little more information on the kind of meeting he would be holding. But this would have to do.

Jim and Kate were leaving when she took her case back to the car, and Ron gave a low whistle. "Wow! I'm surprised Pasetti hasn't signed you as one of his top models."

She waved aside his compliment. "I thought you two guys came together," she said, gesturing toward Jim who was helping Kate into his car.

Ron's grin was contagious. "Nope, I drove. . .just in case I came across some gorgeous woman who needed a ride home. How about it, Amber?"

"Thanks, Ron, but I have my own car."

Apparently he wasn't going to give up easily. "One of us could follow the other, and we could go somewhere for coffee or a nightcap. Or even dancing?"

Amber had to laugh at the ridiculous pose he made, arms poised above his head like the flamenco dancer. "Maybe some other time, Ron. I have to do some work for Mr. Pasetti before I leave."

Ron looked disappointed, but added quickly, "Have time for a turn in the gardens?"

"Sure. He hasn't called for me yet, and I should be able to hear him when he does."

With the approaching dusk, lights had been turned on—thousands, it seemed—miniature stars twinkling from the trees and lamps positioned throughout the grounds. To add to the aura of fantasy, the lamps shimmered with halos created by a mist drifting in from the ocean.

"How long have you been with Pasetti, Ron?"

"About six months." He slowed his stride to match hers. His shirt, a pale blue, brought out the color of his eyes. "I'd never had any intention of becoming a model. But a scout noticed me when I escorted the homecoming queen during football season my last year in college." He grinned. "It's not too bad. A pretty lucrative business, considering the other jobs out there. . .and there are perks, like meeting other models. . .of the feminine persuasion." He slanted her a mischievous look. "Are you sure you're not one of us?"

"Very sure. I'm just a secretary—which reminds me, I'd better see if Mr. Pasetti needs me now."

The crowd had thinned and as Ron began to move away reluctantly, she returned to the patio. Just as Lynn had told her, the hired caterers had missed a few stray cups and glasses, and she picked them up to stow in a huge trash bag.

Gina was the last to leave. The redhead stood very close to Anton as she told him good night, her green eyes almost begging for an invitation to stay. But he laughed down at her good-naturedly and, drawing her hand through his arm, moved toward the arcade and the parking area.

On their way past Amber, Gina hissed, "Better get home and get your beauty sleep, honey. Anton expects his little secretaries to be fresh and dewy-eyed."

Amber bristled and bit back a sharp retort. The woman was impossible! *A gentle answer turns away wrath! A gentle answer turns away wrath!* she quoted Proverbs 15:1 furiously to herself, then managed a halfway genuine smile. "Good night, Gina."

"I could have helped you, Anton," the redhead pouted.

"And dirty those beautiful hands? Not if I can help it. I need you for that important hand lotion campaign, remember?"

Gina's answering smile was radiant.

Amber had to hand it to her boss. He knew how to let a girl down easy.

Still, Gina lost no time. Catching up with Ron, she slipped her arm through his. "Ronnie, darling," she purred, "would you walk me to my car?"

"Sure thing." He waved to the others and he and Gina took off.

As soon as they were out of sight, Anton turned to Amber, his manner suddenly stiff and formal. "There's really no need for you to stay. If you'd rather leave with Ron, you're free to do so."

"But what about your...business? I thought there might be a meeting."

For a moment Anton looked puzzled. "Business?" Dawning awareness crossed his features, and he replied with amusement. "We have just conducted our business, Amber. Meeting adjourned."

Amber stared at him. He seemed to be enjoying himself immensely. Then it struck her. "You mean...?" she gasped, spreading her hands helplessly. "You mean you used *me*...to make Gina jealous?"

His grin broadened, and he threw back his head and laughed heartily.

Amber clenched her fists. Lips taut, she struggled to control the cold, creeping rage that threatened to engulf her. "Mr. Pasetti," she said icily, surprised at the steadiness of her voice, "pardon me if I fail to see the humor in this. Your personal life is your own business. But when you begin to use other people for your little games. . . ."

He took a step toward her, holding out his hands in a conciliatory gesture. "Forgive me if I've offended you. But all's fair in love and war."

Afraid he might touch her, she quickly turned away. Her skirt swirled about her legs as she went to the fountain and sat on the edge of the wall surrounding it.

"If those lions were not made of marble, I do believe they'd flee for their lives," he said, walking over to stand in front of her.

Jumping to her feet, Amber was about to brush past him to leave. But he anticipated the move and his hand shot out, grasping her arm in a firm grip. "Why does it matter so much, Amber?"

The truth doused her anger like a blast of water on a fire. She felt suddenly drained and void of emotion, except for her trembling legs and a pounding pulse.

Did it matter? Perhaps not. Hadn't she sensed that he was the kind of man who thought of women as trophies to be added to his collection? It was wishful thinking to believe otherwise.

"Before I leave, Mr. Pasetti, I want you to understand what I think of your. . .juvenile games. I may be younger than you, but I feel it only fair to warn you that I refuse to work—"

"Miss Jennings!" he exploded, taking hold of both her arms and preventing her escape.

His captive, at least for the moment, Amber stood in front of him, chest heaving. She had hoped to quit her job before he fired her. But now—

"You've said quite enough," he warned. "We're not at the office now. We're just a man and woman trying to have a conversation. And this thing about your being young won't wash. You're all grown up now and, from my observations, wise beyond your years."

"Let me go."

Ignoring her request, he continued, his voice carefully controlled. "It would seem, *Miss* Jennings, that we are two of a kind."

She could only gasp. How dare he think they were anything at all alike!

"Ah," he smirked, "you think I can't see through you? Whom do you think you're kidding, little Miss Innocent? If you're going to accuse me of playing games with Gina, then perhaps I should remind you that your own actions have been highly questionable."

Amber blinked as he went on. "You came to my agency, sporting an engagement ring from a fiancé who—we later learn—is deceased. When I was finally told the true circumstances, you seemed not at all concerned about your loss, only about the job. I decided right then, Miss Jennings, that you had never really been in love."

How could he possibly know that? She had barely admitted it to herself! She lowered her eyes, feeling the quick sting of moisture behind them.

He wasn't through with her. "Then you worked on the sympathy of the entire agency, allowing them to believe you were grieving over your fiancé. Yet today you spent an entire afternoon and evening with Ron Jordan, a man you scarcely know."

Searching her mind for a way to redeem herself,

Amber was speechless.

"And what about the remark Leonard Lamarr made about your eyes? You know he's in the makeup business. Is that why you cozied up to him, calling him by his first name? And right in front of his wife, too! Have you been using your job—and *me,* for that matter—in order to break into modeling?"

"That's not true! I have never—" she choked out, her words barely audible.

"Never?" he asked curiously.

Her gaze lifted to his, drawn into the dark depths against her will. She felt as if her heart would stop. *Please, Lord, don't let him try to kiss me!*

She closed her eyes, feeling a wave of dizziness sweep over her. When she went limp in his arms, he tightened his grasp, then released her. "I'm sorry. I didn't mean to hurt you."

Feeling her legs about to give way, she sank down again onto the wall of the fountain.

"It seems we've arrived at a stalemate, Amber," he said, his voice husky. "You've made accusations against me, and I against you. You say I'm wrong. Maybe so. Maybe I've misjudged you. But that could go both ways, you know. It's possible that you've misjudged me, too."

She felt his assessing look, but could not bring herself to look up at him. His next comment was almost amiable. "Could be you'll discover I'm not such a bad guy, after all."

Hadn't she reached that conclusion herself not very long ago? But that was before—

He dropped down beside her and took her hand. She

was too stunned to resist. His words, his fingers caressing her knuckles were hypnotic. She hadn't the faintest idea what to believe anymore. Did he truly think she was devious, a woman with ulterior motives? If so, why was he still trying to make another conquest? Or was it just that he was the ultimate con artist?

He released her hand, then stood, pulling her to her feet. His smile was beguiling, his eyes filled with sincerity. "Let's start over, Amber, without the distrust, the suspicions. You let go of your preconceived notions about me, and I'll ask you to forgive me for accusing you unjustly."

Amber hugged her arms to herself, feeling chilled in the cool night air. How could she make such a deal with him? Everything he'd said about her was *not* untrue. And she couldn't help but be suspicious of him still because he had asked her to stay under obviously false pretenses.

And yet, she wasn't up to another verbal battle. Before she had an inkling of how to respond, he asked softly, "Couldn't we be friends?"

Friends? After tonight, she wasn't sure. But she *could* answer honestly, "We haven't had any problems at the office."

"True," he replied. "But I'm speaking of after office hours, when you're not an employee but a beautiful young woman, whose eyes seem to reach inside the soul, whose sweet lips are made for kissing, and whose soft, southern drawl melts the heart."

She caught her breath. He was playing games again. That line was straight out of some movie. She turned away. He was wrong about one thing—she was not wise beyond her years, not wise at all. "I'm afraid our lifestyles are too different for there to be anything for us outside the office," she said, then added, moving toward her car, "Good night, Mr. Pasetti."

His next words stopped her in her tracks. "Different . . .because you're a Christian?" She didn't move. "I'd like to talk to you about that. It's one reason I asked you to stay tonight."

How clever of him. If he knew anything at all about Christianity, he would know there was no way she could refuse such a request. She turned her head slowly.

She had never been so frightened in her life. She was afraid of his clever tricks, his quick wit. Afraid of her own vulnerability. She breathed a quick, silent prayer.

Then Anton was beside her, holding out his hand. "We'll talk," he said gently. "But first, like the pompous, arrogant materialist I am, I'd like to show you my home."

seven

Anton steered Amber through the house, describing each room in detail. She tried to forget the incident at the fountain, tried instead to concentrate on the gleaming tiled floors and rich carpets. Light from ornate chandeliers glowed softly, illuminating the many paintings lining the wide hallways.

"An El Greco!" she burst out, forgetting everything else in her delight.

He slanted her a sidelong glance, then back at the painting. "My mother's favorite," he explained. " 'Adoration of the Shepherds.' But you know the painting as well as the artist, of course."

"Of course." So she had caught *him* off guard, for a change. "I know his style. He's famous for painting elongated figures."

"Some critics say he was mad," Anton put in, testing her.

"Others say he had bad eyesight," Amber returned, then cut her eyes around at him. He seemed amused—and pleased. But she was no connoisseur of the arts, hadn't traveled widely or trained extensively. He would know that anyway; her resumé spelled out her business school education and her family background. A small town would not be likely to provide the rich opportunities that were a natural part of his heritage.

"Two semesters of Art History at the University of Asheville." She ducked her head, then looked up at him with a contrite expression.

Now that he was smiling at her, blue glints sparking his smoky eyes, she dared to take it a step further. "Another reason I remember El Greco is because he spent most of his life in Toledo. At first," she admitted sheepishly, "I thought the biographer was talking about Toledo, Ohio. . . not Spain!"

"Art History was not my best subject, either, Amber. Seems *I* thought it was. . .an irreverent expression!" He seemed to reconsider telling her just what he meant by that.

They smiled at each other, and she felt no qualms at all this time in accepting his offer to continue the tour.

By the grand stairway, Anton stopped before a pair of portraits. "My mother and father."

The dark-haired woman reminded Amber of the beautiful Spanish dancer she had seen earlier that evening. The eyes in the portrait, however, were not those of a flirt, but of a warm-hearted, gracious lady. Next to her portrait hung that of a ruggedly handsome man, his chiseled features softened by light brown hair that fell in soft waves from a center part.

Anton's golden bronze complexion and dark coloring were obviously from his mother's side of the family, while his stature was probably from his father's side. She risked a glance at him and caught him staring at his mother's picture. A man who loved his mother—and wasn't ashamed to show it.

As if suddenly aware of the tense silence, Anton started up his tour guide monologue. "This wing," he gestured toward the front of the house," living room, salon, formal dining room, ballroom, is used primarily for entertaining. You've seen most of that. Since it would take much too long to explore the entire house, I'll take you through the living quarters."

Anton had implied that his personal quarters were small and informal compared to the more public areas, but Amber was stunned by their size and elegance. In the dining room, the walnut table and chairs hardly seemed informal to her, nor the lavish ornamentation and lovely rich colors of the Oriental rugs used in the rooms. The living room furniture—covered in suedes, velvets, and leather—repeated the deep reds, golds, blues, and emerald greens of the carpet.

"Many of the furnishings are contemporary," Anton explained, "but Mother was partial to the Mediterranean influence."

"It's breathtaking."

They returned to the hallway, and Anton led her up the stairs that spiraled up to yet another floor. As they walked along the landing, she could look down on the first floor, where the crystal chandelier cast diamond-shaped patterns of light onto the tiles below.

"The doors to the right lead to suites," Anton pointed out, "but this is my favorite." Stepping forward, he opened a door on their left.

Amber walked into a very masculine study with leather couches and overstuffed chairs, dark paneled walls, floor-to-ceiling bookcases, and a walk-in fireplace. He pulled a cord at the side of the deep red velvet draperies under Moorish arches, and the draperies parted, exposing glass doors, and on the other side, a balcony protected by a black wrought-iron railing.

Anton slid open the glass doors, and they walked out onto the balcony, breathing in the cool night air. At one side was a garden table and chairs. As if on cue, an elevator door opened onto the balcony and a uniformed servant trundled a wheeled cart over to the table. Anton pulled out a chair for Amber.

The servant poured coffee and set a tray of delicate pastries on the table, then lit two candles in heavy, silver candlesticks. "Thank you, Mitchell. That will be all." Anton dismissed him with a nod.

Amber took a sip of the hot coffee, then picked up a pastry. Avoiding Anton's gaze, she looked down at the formal gardens below. She was very near tears. It had been a long day, and her emotions had taken a roller coaster ride. Now the very peace and tranquillity of this place was almost too much.

Anton was waiting. She really ought to say something. A Pasetti employee was always cool and collected, always knew the right thing to say. "Well, Amber?"

It might not be the Pasetti way, but she could only be honest. "I feel. . ." she hesitated and allowed herself to lock onto his gaze. Funny. The candlelight was reflected in his eyes, making them glisten with a silvery sheen. Then a breeze stirred, and the candle guttered and almost died, shadowing the strong planes of his face. "I feel as if. . .as if I've been introduced to your mother."

In the silence that followed, she wondered if she had offended him by bringing up a painful subject.

At last he spoke up. "I've had many compliments on this house and grounds. . .but no one has ever said a thing like that before." He regarded her thoughtfully, and she felt another prickle of apprehension. "You are a very perceptive young woman. All of this," he said, with an encompassing sweep of his hand, "is a product of my mother's good taste and perseverance. My father would have lost everything through his gambling and drinking if Mother hadn't taken over and kept the business going. I watched her struggle. After my father died, she continued to carry on. . .without much help from me, I'm afraid." He gave a bitter laugh and picked up a heavily carved silver spoon, twirling it as he went on. "I've often regretted the time I spent abroad instead of staying her to help her," he sighed, "but I was young and impulsive. . .and stubborn."

Amber forgot that he was her employer, as he told of the cancer that had destroyed by inches what had once been a vital and beautiful woman. There were tears in his eyes when he looked up. "But the illness brought her closer to her God. That's when she designed the house, using the architecture of a Spanish mission and installed the bell tower, where the carillon plays at dusk each day. Her idea was that in those few moments, at least, the faithful should remember their Creator. I'll show it to you some time. On a clear day, you can see our private beach from there." He choked. "Mother used to shoo me away from her bedside to go there when the suffering became too great, saying she could signal me with the bell if she needed me. She lived four long years like that."

It was all Amber could do to restrain herself from putting out a hand to comfort him. But he had not finished.

"It was during my mother's years of illness that I began to grow up. . .assume more responsibility for the business. I promised to keep the business going. But she laid the groundwork for our success. I simply inherited the results of her hard work."

Stunned by this revelation, Amber could only sit, allowing him to absorb the peace of the evening. Finally, she ventured a comment. "You work very hard, too," she said softly. "I'm sure your mother would be very proud of you."

He let out a long sigh. "Yes, I can feel a sense of accomplishment in that, at least. But it was my mother who set the pace. This house reflects her tastes, her spirit. . . though I suppose someday my wife will make some changes, add her own touches to the place."

His *wife*. Amber wondered if Gina would be the next Mrs. Pasetti.

Anton's voice was quiet in the stillness, a stillness strangely enhanced by the distant lapping of waves against the shoreline. "It was my mother who taught me that possessions are cold and impersonal, totally without meaning. . .unless there is someone to share them. She was right."

"Your mother. . .was wise as well as beautiful."

"She'll always be a part of me." He lifted his head and narrowed his gaze speculatively. "It's good to remember those we have loved. . .but there comes a time when we must face the fact that life goes on and we have other duties and obligations to the world. . .and to ourselves."

Amber shivered slightly in the evening breeze. Was he going to ask her about Ken?

"My mother had a way of accepting whatever came as God's Will," Anton went on. "When she was too weak to hold her Bible, I sat beside her bed and read to her for hours." His tone was laced with pain as he lifted the silver chain at his throat.

For the first time, Amber noticed a small cross attached. She had to know. "Are you a Christian then, Mr. Pasetti?"

He shook his head. "No. . .I wear this cross in her memory. Oh, I tried it. When the pain seemed unbearable, I asked that unseen God of hers to give her peace . . .to take her pain away. . .or release her in death." Anton regarded Amber with such intensity that she knew he was speaking the truth. "When neither prayer was answered." He shrugged, then spat bitterly, "How could I trust in a God Who would allow such suffering?"

Amber squirmed under his penetrating gaze. She understood his confusion, his frustration. "Sometimes I've wondered, too, where is God?" she admitted. "Why does He allow such terrible things to happen? Why did He let a boating accident take my parents from me when I was only seven? On the other hand, if God stepped in to prevent all evil, then we'd be nothing more than puppets. What father wants his children to love and obey him because they have no other choice?"

Anton was still studying her, watching, waiting, as if nothing she had said so far had registered with him. She rushed to her conclusion. "At least, with God's help, we can get through painful times. We can know that someday, either here on earth or in heaven, everything will be all right."

Anton snapped out of his reverie. "Oh, so God is a *crutch*," he said, his voice tinged with skepticism.

Amber hesitated only a moment. "If you had a broken leg, you'd use a crutch, wouldn't you?"

He nodded, somewhat reluctantly, she thought. "And we are broken, twisted, weak inside. *All* of us," she added pointedly.

Her words apparently did not faze him. Instead, he shifted

the subject. "Amber, you lost the man you were going to marry. You might say God took him. Why?"

Amber averted her eyes. "I. . .really don't know. But I do know that God has a plan for me. . .either with or without a husband. I'll just wait until He leads me to the right man."

"And of course that man will have to be a *Christian* to be a real man in your eyes." There was no mistaking the sarcasm edging his remark.

Amber picked up her spoon and stirred the half cup of coffee that didn't need stirring. The ensuing silence was loaded. Whatever she said now could make or break their tenuous relationship. But she wasn't about to lie!

Still, she wasn't expecting his next comment, delivered as nonchalantly as if he were speculating on the weather. "I wonder what God would do for me, if I became a Christian."

"Maybe nothing you *think* you want. But you can be sure it would be best." She couldn't believe she had spoken so boldly—to Anton Pasetti, of all people!

"Your honesty is. . .quite refreshing. It's one of the things I've come to admire about you."

"I guess I *am* blunt sometimes," she admitted. "And I also have a temper."

"So I've noticed." His serious demeanor gave way to a slow grin. "Some women are even more beautiful when they're angry."

Her wariness surfaced again. He was probably thinking of Gina. But he really shouldn't be talking this way. Still, he might just be testing her. Or maybe this whole conversation had been a ploy to add her to his collection.

She had to admit she was beginning to feel as human as the million and one other women who found Anton Pasetti attractive. She was determined, however, that he would be the last to find out. "I really should go," she said, keeping her voice—if not the rest of her—coolly detached.

He was on his feet instantly. Probably he had just been waiting for her to leave so he could call Gina. It was still early.

"Let's take the elevator." He led the way to the corner of the balcony where he pressed a button beside a pair of recessed doors.

When they slid open, he motioned her inside. At the bottom, they stepped into an alcove off the kitchen. Mitchell was sitting at a table drinking coffee, while a couple of uniformed women were putting dishes away.

"Mitchell, would you follow us in Amber's car, then drive me back?" Anton asked.

"Oh, I wouldn't want to put Mr. Mitchell to any trouble," Amber protested.

"You know your way around these freeways?"

"Not too well," she had to admit. "Maybe if you just gave me directions. . . ."

The women had stopped their work and were staring openly. Mitchell looked embarrassed. . .or sympathetic, she couldn't tell which. She saw the glance he gave Anton, whose smug look resembled that of the cat who swallowed the canary.

"Your keys, please," Anton said.

Amber fished them from her purse and handed them over. "Come along." Anton slipped her keys to Mitchell, then guided her, with a light touch at the small of her back, out to his car in the garage.

Without a word, she followed the deft movements of his hands as he steered the big Mercedes out of the garage, whipped it around, and turned toward town.

From the passenger's side, Amber looked out the window. The seascape spreading across her line of vision was black velvet studded with diamonds, mirroring the night sky. Here and there a froth of white—like lace—rode in on the waves as they rolled to the shore. For several moments neither one of them said a word as they drove through the night.

"You and Ron Jordan seemed to hit it off rather well," Anton said when he finally broke the silence.

Amber hadn't given Ron another thought, but now she recalled that he and Gina had left together. Was Anton jealous? How ironic if his plan had backfired.

When she didn't comment, he continued. "The night is young. If you'd left with Ron and the others, you'd probably be out there, too." He gestured toward the beach, where several cars had pulled off to park.

Amber still didn't speak, but she kept her head turned toward the ocean. He was right. But for some reason she did not regret the evening spent at Anton Pasetti's house.

With a flick of his wrist, Anton wheeled the car off the road and parked on the sand near the other cars. Over her shoulder, Amber could see Mitchell pulling up in her little blue car, a short distance behind them.

"Shall we walk on the beach?" Anton asked, apparently amused at her wide-eyed expression.

Amber cleared her throat nervously. "I can't walk very far in these heels. But I did bring along another pair."

She retrieved them from her bag and put them on, not sure what her boss planned to do next.

He stood quietly, studying the moon-washed shore. "It's

been a long time since I've seen the beach at night. . .in the company of a young woman."

Now that *was* a surprise!

The sea breeze felt good on her flushed face as he reached out to tug her along, steadying her in the shifting sand. From here, they could see several couples playing in the water. Others walked along the beach, hand in hand, while some sat on blankets, locked in romantic embraces.

They hadn't walked very far when Anton stopped and turned to face her. She felt as if the surf were pounding in her ears as he tilted her chin upward with his thumb and forefinger. "Is this what Ron would have done?"

"Oh, he'd probably have thrown me in the ocean!" she quipped, hoping to dispel the sudden tension between them.

Anton's mood did not alter. "Then he would have rescued the lovely damsel in distress. . .and kissed her?"

"Oh, I doubt that!" She laughed uneasily and twisted out of his grasp, not daring to look into those eyes, luring her into their dark depths. She chafed her arms where goosebumps were blossoming. "It's chilly out here. We'd better leave."

Anton shrugged and led her back to the car. She was relieved when he started up the engine immediately, then switched on the radio. There was no need for conversation, other than the necessary instructions to her cottage.

When they arrived at the motor court, she motioned to Mitchell to park under the palm tree, then waited while Anton pulled the Mercedes in behind her Escort.

Without waiting for Anton, Amber hopped out of the car and hurried over to the butler. "Thank you, Mr. Mitchell. I hope this hasn't inconvenienced you too much."

He bowed formally, but his smile was warm. "Not at all, miss."

Anton took the key from her and unlocked the back door. She switched on the kitchen light, and they stepped inside. At least she hadn't left dirty dishes in the sink!

"Check to see if everything is all right."

He's always bossing people around, she thought, but she kept her thoughts to herself. Still feeling awkward, she attempted a joke. "There's nothing here anyone would want."

When he didn't budge, she made a quick inspection, then reported back to the kitchen. "All's well." She held out her hand for him to shake. "Thank you for a beautiful day."

But it was not a handshake he gave her. He lifted her hand to his lips and planted a light kiss before releasing it. She felt a tingle of pleasure, then reminded herself that it didn't mean anything. Even Len Lamarr had kissed her hand. Must be another Pasetti thing.

"Glad you enjoyed the picnic. . .at least some of it, anyway. Good night."

He melted into the darkness before she could catch her breath. "Good night," she called after him.

She locked the door, then leaned against it, listening to his footsteps retreating down the gravel driveway, then the soft hum of the Mercedes as Mitchell backed and drove away.

She stared down at her hand where he had branded it with his lips. Like a silly schoolgirl, she considered never washing it again. His cologne lingered in the air—subtle, yet stirringly masculine.

Tonight she'd seen another side of Anton Pasetti. . .and had *felt* an unexpected side of herself. She wasn't at all sure what to do about either one.

eight

On Sunday morning the shrill of the phone blasted away the last remnant of Amber's dreams. She sat up, every sense instantly alert. Anton?

But it was Ron. "How does a trip to Tijuana sound to you?" *How can any human being sound so cheerful so early in the morning?* she grumbled to herself. "With Kate and Jim?" he went on.

"I'm. . .barely awake," she said, stifling a yawn—and her disappointment. "I didn't set my alarm."

"Have your coffee and we'll pick you up in about an hour."

"Wait a minute! Let me think." She swung her legs over the side of the bed and grabbed for her robe. "Why don't you three join me for church and we could go afterward."

There was a brief pause. "If those are your terms. . . sure. You have yourself a deal. I'll tell the others."

"The church is on the beach front. . .strictly casual for tourists," she said. "So we can dress for Mexico and leave from there."

Amber took her time getting ready. She washed her hair in the shower, then wrapped it in a towel, turban-style, while she sat at her tiny kitchen window, looking out on her own "formal" gardens—one lonely palm—and sipping a cup of coffee. Had last night been a dream? Had

she really spent time alone with the most eligible bachelor
in San Diego?

Amber forced her thoughts from *then* to *now*. Maybe
she shouldn't have cut a deal about going to church. But
whatever worked.

So far, only Kate had ever gone with her to the beachfront church, and not every Sunday at that. Why was it
she seemed doomed to failure when it came to sharing
her faith? Like last night, when Anton Pasetti had confessed that he'd tried to bargain with God. Thinking back
to her answer, she flinched. She'd come off sounding like
a Pollyanna. He probably thought she was hopelessly un-
sophisticated and had turned her off without hearing a word
she'd tried to say.

But then his beloved mother had tried, too, and although
he apparently loved and respected her greatly, she hadn't
succeeded in leading him to Christ, either.

Glancing at the kitchen clock, Amber took her cup to
the sink, then padded back to the bedroom. She chose a
yellow pants outfit, then tied her nearly dry hair back with
a yellow ribbon. The natural curl would spring into shape
without much coaxing. At least, she had that much for
which to be thankful.

Since she'd be in the sun most of the day, she applied a
light makeup base with sunscreen, a little lip gloss, and a
touch of mascara. There. That should take care of the
outside. She wrinkled her nose at her reflection.

When she heard Ron's car in the driveway, she hurried
out to meet him.

He gave a low whistle when he saw her. "You look like
sunshine on a summer morning. And take a look at this

weather. Not a cloud in the sky. It's going to be a great day!"

Amber slid into the front seat of Ron's Mustang and turned to speak to Kate and Jim in the back seat. Even though Kate had been attractive when they'd first met, she was positively glowing these days. *That's not entirely due to Pasetti magic,* Amber knew. *I think Jim has a lot to do with it.*

Still, she was concerned that her new friends didn't glow with the joy of the Lord. Even Anton knew that, with all his beautiful possessions—including his women—life could be empty. During the church service, he and her friends were on her mind like a ceaseless prayer.

ও

Right after the service, they headed for the border, ready for a day of fun. As they strolled through the Mexican tourist town, the four of them laughed and joked, and weren't too particular about what they ate.

"Junk food once in a while won't kill us. . .I hope." Kate made a face and popped a burrito into her mouth.

For a while, they could forget they were products of the Pasetti Agency. But it all came back when Ron bought two wide-brimmed sombreros and plopped one on Amber's head.

"Souvenir," he explained, covering his own blond hair with the other. Amber suspected he was conscious of the bright sun on his fair skin.

Jim did the same. "Wouldn't want Pasetti women to burn their pretty little noses," he said, adjusting Kate's hat, then tweaking her pretty little nose.

Getting into the festive mood of the day, Amber splurged

and bought a Mexican skirt and blouse from a street vendor. Ron presented her with some heavy, outrageously colorful Mexican jewelry.

"I dare you to wear that getup to work tomorrow," Kate said, mischief sparking her big, round eyes.

"I'll do it!" Amber couldn't believe she'd said that. But as the day wore on, her natural reserve just seemed to melt away. Once, when she was alone with Kate for a minute, she even opened up enough to tell her friend her deepest secret—that she hadn't loved Ken as much as she thought she ought to love the man she was going to marry.

"You shouldn't feel guilty about that," Kate chided. "Look how many people think they're in love, then their marriages break up. But," she dropped her voice to an excited whisper, "I think Jim might be the one for me. Would you believe we knew each other in junior high school—back when our dads were in Annapolis? Except I was a scrawny thirteen-year-old girl and he wasn't the hunk he is today!"

Amber felt much better after her confession. . .and Kate's announcement. In fact, she even allowed Ron to kiss her good night when they returned late that evening, regretting it almost immediately. She'd have to make it very clear to him that she wasn't ready to consider anything more than friendship.

ঌ

By Monday morning she was also regretting having accepted Kate's dare. "How do I get myself into these things?" she grumbled. "Still, a promise is a promise."

But not until she arrived at work did she realize she

might have made a huge mistake. She was at the coffee urn, just starting to pour a cup, when Anton walked in and stopped abruptly.

Amber cringed as his gaze raked her from head to toe. She could only imagine what he must be thinking as he observed the sight she made: Hair pulled back on one side to expose the dangling earring that matched her flamboyant necklace; off-the-shoulder peasant blouse; full black skirt, hand-painted with brilliant peacocks; black high-heeled sandals. Even her complexion, kissed by the weekend sun, had darkened a shade. She must look like a gypsy!

Anton strode toward her, and she backed away until there was nowhere else to go.

"Tijuana special?" he asked, trapping her between himself and the wall. He touched the bauble at her ear. "Cute."

Granted, she was not dressed properly for the office. But in spite of her trembling lips, she managed to defend herself. "The jewelry was a *gift*. It's only courteous to show one's appreciation, isn't it? Even Pasetti philosophy teaches us to consider the feelings of others."

"So this is all compliments of the generous Mr. Jordan?" His eyes swept over her again.

"Just the jewelry," she put in hastily. "I bought the rest myself. But I wore it. . .on a dare. I'll go change." Not meeting his eyes, she tried to duck around him, when his tone halted her in her tracks.

"Miss Jennings! You're. . .not. . .going. . .anywhere."

Surprised, she looked up to see a smile tugging at one corner of his mouth. "You're fine just as you are. It's only that, after seeing you, I'm wondering whether I'll get any work out of my male employees today." He broke into a grin and then a chuckle.

"What's going on here?" Charis wanted to know when she heard the laughter and stepped into the room. One glimpse of Amber brought a gasp. "Amber Jennings, is that *you?*"

Anton answered for her. "Yes indeed, would you believe that beneath all that cool competence beats the fiery heart of a Spanish señorita?" With one last appraising look, he turned and walked into his office.

Amber stared at the door that closed firmly behind him. *Cool?* Ha! Hadn't he guessed how often he'd left her uncomfortably *warm?* To the boiling point, to be exact!

She sighed. "I really goofed, didn't I, Charis?"

The older woman looked sympathetic. "Well, I wouldn't make a practice of wearing costumes to the office. But since you did, I'm glad you chose this particular outfit. Nothing Mexican or Spanish would offend Anton." Her lovely face broke into a smile. "You know, Amber, sometimes it's good for a woman, no matter how beautiful, to break out of her mold. Makes a man sit up and take notice."

"Oh, but I wasn't trying—"

"Oh, of *course* not." With a speculative glance out of the corner of her eye, Charis breezed out of the office, her final comment trailing over her shoulder. "But you accomplished it just the same."

≈

It didn't take long for others in the building to notice Amber's new look. The men were openly admiring, while the other women were either complimentary, catty, or critical. As Charis put it later, "Without the Lord in their hearts, they can't understand the concept of rejoicing in other people's successes."

When Amber ran into Ron in the cafeteria, his mouth dropped open. "Wow! Is this the same woman who went south of the border with me last weekend?" But she had to turn him down when he asked her out for the following weekend. Better not encourage him, lest she drift into the same dead-end pattern that had made her so miserable with Ken.

Anton Pasetti, on the other hand, was all business for the remainder of the day. Even when he summoned her to discuss the minutes of the last board meeting, he acted as if their intimate talk at his home and their morning encounter had never taken place.

In fact, he paid her no attention at all until he walked out of his office at closing time. Pausing, with his hand on the knob of the outer door, he winked. "Good night, señorita."

&

The following day, Anton informed Amber that he and Gina would be leaving for New York for a week or so, in connection with the shampoo contract. And during the next few days, he was completely preoccupied with details of the upcoming trip.

"The reservations are made?" he asked on one occasion.

Amber nodded. "Yes, sir. Everything's ready." She had all the information at her fingertips: airline tickets, adjoining room reservations for him and Gina at the hotel in New York, and a schedule of appointments.

On Wednesday, the day of departure, Anton paused at Amber's desk. "I need to see you. . .in the coffee shop." His brusque, businesslike tone matched his dark suit.

Automatically, she dialed Charis's number and requested

a secretary from the pool to cover her desk. Then she pulled up the file her boss would undoubtedly want to review and printed out a copy.

They stepped into the elevator and the door closed. For some reason, even though there were only two of them inside, the small enclosure seemed more cramped than usual. She was relieved when they reached their floor.

With a light touch under her elbow, he guided her to a booth. Her skin tingled beneath the honey-colored fabric of her sleeve. But his gesture was, of course, entirely proper. He was, after all, the boss and she, his employee.

Settling herself in the booth, she glanced at Anton, wondering if she would ever get used to his proprietary manner. He had *hired* her; he didn't *own* her! Still, he probably subjected all his employees to the kind of scrutiny he was giving her now. Probably wanted to make sure she was measuring up to agency expectations. But it was more than a little disconcerting.

Anton ordered coffee for them and Amber opened the file.

"What's that?" he asked.

"The file on your trip, Mr. Pasetti. I have a copy of everything and a schedule complete with times, places, and contact people."

"The woman never lets me down," he mumbled to himself. "Now close that file. Just make sure you put it in my briefcase before I leave."

She eyed him questioningly. His smile was relaxed, not at all professional. . .but friendly. Gone was the preoccupied expression of the past few days. Amber could handle his office manner, but this? She was grateful when the waitress brought their coffee and set it in front of them. She concentrated on the swirl of steam rising from the cup while Anton stirred cream into his.

"I don't mind hard work," she said, lifting the cup to her lips and taking a careful sip.

"You've proven your point. But the workload shouldn't be as heavy while I'm away."

What did he expect her to say? "Of course," Amber replied lightly, and glanced around the near-empty room. "You know that old saying: 'When the cat's away, the mice will play.'"

Anton laughed. "Not you, Amber. But promise me you *will* take some time off."

Amber hesitated. Was this another test? "I prefer work to boredom."

"Boredom?" He cocked a brow. "What about all your young friends?"

She could have bitten her tongue! Why had she brought up the subject? But there was no way she was going to explain that she was trying to hold Ron at bay, and that Kate and Jim were so absorbed in each other, that Amber barely saw her best friend these days.

"Feel free to use my house. . .the gardens. . .my private beach. Mitchell or one of the maids could show you around. As you know, it's quite secluded if you want to be alone. Or, if you prefer, you might entertain your. . .friends. I suppose you're still seeing Ron Jordan?"

"Not often."

"Getting too serious, was he?" Anton didn't wait for an answer. "You keep a tight rein on your emotions, don't you, Amber?"

She didn't look at him. "I'm all right." Her boss was probably only concerned about an employee who wasn't leading what he considered a "normal" life. And to a man like Anton Pasetti, that included intimacy with the opposite sex.

Yet it was not Ron's kiss she sometimes dreamed about, but the burning light pressure of Anton's lips on the back of her hand.

"I do hope you are. . .all right, Amber." Anton's voice was soft, gentle. "I value you very highly, you know."

Feeling his gaze on her in the uncomfortable silence, Amber could not trust herself to look at him. Unconsciously she lifted her arm and glanced at her watch, then quickly lowered it.

"There's no rush, Amber." Anton chuckled. "I'm the boss, remember?"

That's one thing I try never to forget, she was thinking and made a feeble attempt to laugh. A man and his secretary should be able to have a cup of coffee together without stress.

"Do you like New York, Mr. Pasetti?" she asked, trying for a casual tone.

"Very much. The pace is even more hectic than in California, believe it or not. But I thrive on activity. One has the sense of accomplishment, of getting things done." There was a small, secretive smile. "Still, there *are* evenings, after a busy day, when there is time to gaze out of a window far above the city and watch the traffic below. Up there, it's a whole new world."

Caught up in his mood, she sighed. "Sounds romantic."

"Only if one isn't alone."

Well, he certainly wouldn't be alone. Gina would be

with him. Amber dabbed at her lips with the napkin. "I'm sure you'll enjoy your trip."

"Much like you," he was saying, "I find pleasure in work. But I've learned the art of relaxation, as well. I wonder if *you* have."

"You have enough to do without worrying about me," she retorted, took a sip of the coffee, and grimaced. It was cold.

"I do worry about you, Amber," he said suddenly, leaning forward. "I sense that something is closed off in that interesting mind of yours. Now, while I'm away, you take it easy. That's an order."

Amber responded to his playful tone with a little salute. "Yes, *sir!*"

"Good. Ready to go?"

She nodded and picked up the file. They walked out of the coffee shop and back toward the elevator. Inside the cubicle, Amber watched the lighted buttons registering the floors as they passed—3. . .4. . .5. . .6. . .7. . .8. Instead of stopping on the eighth floor, however, she was amazed to see the buttons blinking on all the way to the fifteenth.

As the doors opened, Anton motioned her forward with a nod of his head. She stepped out into a carpeted hallway. "My apartments," he said. "For the sake of convenience, I often stay here after a late night with a client. Sometimes I conduct business here."

I'll just bet you do, Amber thought.

He led her through a huge living room, up several steps, and through another doorway that opened onto a rooftop garden.

She couldn't restrain a gasp of pleasure and walked over to look over the edge of a wall. "Oh. . .I didn't realize it would be so far down."

"Heights bother you?" he asked, coming up behind her to steady her with a hand at her waist.

"N-not really. It's just that back home, there wasn't anything this tall—except for the mountains, of course. It's strange, looking straight down like this. The cars look like toys."

"Can't even hear the traffic from here, can we?" He narrowed his gaze. "You have flown, of course."

"No," she admitted, embarrassed. She gave a helpless shrug. "No wings."

He laughed at her little joke. "You'll have to try it some-day. It's the only way to travel."

She looked down again at the traffic far below. "The air must be thinner up here."

"Think so?"

She glanced at him in time to catch the quirk of one eyebrow and the slight smile of amusement playing around his lips. "Well," she said determinedly, "I know it's a little harder to breathe."

"I see," he said. "And you're sure it's *height* that causes that sensation?"

The next moment he had spun her around to face him. She inhaled sharply. Kept her eyes on his tie. Felt the gentle pressure of his hands on her arms. Yes, it was definitely height that caused her breathlessness—but not the height of the building.

"Tell me good-bye, Amber," he said softly. "And please . . .call me Anton."

Before the whispered name was off her lips, his own were pressing against hers. His fingers tightened momentarily and then he released her. Slowly he stepped back and walked over to the door, holding it open for her.

In the elevator again, she floated down to the eighth floor. Time seemed suspended. Had the last few minutes really happened? The door opened and she turned toward the office, with Anton right behind her.

Hold your head up. Walk confidently, she quoted the Pasetti rulebook. *It was only a casual brush of the lips. It's done all the time.*

A shiver tingled down her spine. Who was she kidding? This was Anton Pasetti, king of a dynasty. No woman in her right mind would refuse him a simple farewell kiss. And that's all it was, wasn't it?

❧

For the next hour, Amber worked feverishly, checking and double-checking the file that Anton would take with him. When he was ready to leave, she watched him slide the file into his briefcase. He seemed distracted again, as if the kiss had never occurred.

When Gina came in, he greeted her with a devastating smile. Amber couldn't help thinking how like a cat the redhead appeared. She was positively purring!

Amber watched with a twinge that was very like jealousy as they moved toward the door of her office. Then Anton swiveled on his heel and pointed a finger at Amber. "Remember."

Remember to relax while he was away? Or remember the tender scene in his private garden?

This time his dazzling smile was for Amber. But it was Gina who walked away on his arm.

nine

On Saturday evening, Amber sat on the Lamarrs' terrace, surrounded by exotic shrubs in lavish bloom. The three were sipping minted tea and enjoying the warmth of the evening after a superb dinner.

Amber had felt perfectly at ease in accepting Charis's invitation to their home, a large contemporary as elegant and graceful as the owners. Anton had implied that once one is an adult, there are no longer age distinctions. She felt that the same principle applied to Christians. In her relationship with Charis and Len, there was a bond that transcended any so-called "generation gap."

Even in such congenial company, though, there was a nagging apprehension. Tonight Anton and Gina would meet with the owner of the shampoo firm. Gina would probably land the contract, and then she and Anton would celebrate. *How* they would celebrate, Amber wasn't quite sure. All she knew was that, in matters of the heart, she and Anton Pasetti were poles apart.

Charis's soft voice broke Amber's reverie. "Excuse the interruption, but your mind is undoubtedly miles away, dear."

About two thousand or so, Amber figured. "Oh, I'm sorry!" But she hadn't been daydreaming about North Carolina. Actually, in her mind, she was in New York City, standing above the traffic in a skyscraper among the clouds. The setting was romantic. The man was tall, dark, remarkably attractive. The woman had a riot of red hair and luminous green eyes.

"Well, wherever you are, hold that thought, Amber, my dear," Len put in. "That's exactly the look I'd like to capture for an ad I have in mind. Mysterious. . .haunting. . ."

Amber was startled, then amused. During dinner Len had mentioned something about using her as a model, but she couldn't believe he'd been serious.

She took another sip of her tea and concentrated on what Charis was saying. "I was wondering if you'd like to see an old movie, Amber. It might interest you. Our daughter, Layla, had a part in it."

A daughter? Neither Len nor Charis had ever mentioned children. Amber was curious. "I'd love to."

Len led them into a small room with soft leather couches surrounding three sides. He pulled down a screen on the blank wall, then went to the projection equipment, which apparently was always set up for a showing.

"There she is. That's our Layla." Charis's tone was wistful as a striking young woman came into view. A close-up revealed the same light blue eyes as her mother, and platinum blond hair that curled about an oval face framing small, delicate features.

"What a beautiful young woman." Taking a sidelong glance at Charis in the subdued lighting, Amber thought she detected the glimmer of a tear. What was that all about?

Then, concentrating on the feature-length movie, she lost herself in the story. Even with a bit part, Layla was an impressive actress, and Amber wondered where the an impressive actress, and Amber wondered where the young woman was now.

When the lights came on, Len rose to reset the projector.

"She was our only child," Charis explained in answer to Amber's unspoken question. "She died seven years ago, when she was about your age."

In the next few moments a bittersweet story unfolded, more touching than the movie. The young woman who had had everything—beauty, talent, opportunity. . . "and Anton," Charis finished.

Amber stared. Was that why he had never married? After all these years, was he still in love with Layla?

"They often spoke of marriage," Charis went on. "But Layla was driven to succeed in her career." She paused. "We adored her so. I'm afraid we spoiled her completely."

Len looked up from the projector and leveled a searching look at his wife. "It's pointless, darling, to condemn ourselves."

"I know. . .you keep reminding me that hindsight is a waste of time. But I can't help it, Len. God has forgiven the mistakes we made with our daughter, but there are still lessons to be learned."

Amber suddenly felt that she was eavesdropping on the most intimate conversation between a husband and wife. Their wound was still raw. . .as raw and tender as her own unfortunate engagement to Ken. And now, she was beginning to wonder if she was stumbling into another relationship that would prove just as fatal.

"We gave her everything. . .but the most important thing of all," Charis's eyes were filled with tears, "faith in Jesus

Christ. We didn't know Him ourselves. . .then. Now we'd give anything in the world if we could have her back just long enough to. . . ."

Amber had to look away from the pain in the woman's eyes.

Len went to Charis, cradling her in his arms, comforting her. "We're not sentimentalists living in the past, Amber," he explained over his wife's head. "We just wanted you to know that we understand the cruel blows life can deal. But we've also discovered that God's grace makes it possible. . .to bear such a loss."

How well she knew. "I don't know how people handle those times without faith in God," she added softly, wondering how Anton had survived *two* tragedies without Him.

At last Charis lifted her head. "It was losing Layla that sent Len and me to our knees. We probably would have put it off indefinitely, even with Anton's mother trying to talk sense into us for years. After all, it's not that we didn't believe that there *was* a God. . .we simply didn't trust Him enough to run our lives. . .and our business."

A watery trail of mascara trickled down the older woman's cheek, and she blotted the tears with a tissue. "Maybe the Lord is giving us another chance. . .sending you to us. We've come to care for you very much, Amber. We sense that you're a very private person. . .that you don't open up easily. But if you ever want to talk. . . please know that Len and I are here for you."

Amber didn't know what to say. She was touched, of course. But Charis and Len thought she was still grieving a beloved fiancé. What would they think if they knew the truth?

time, after such a dramatic testimony, to admit that while she regretted losing a dear friend, she was definitely not suffering from a broken heart. "Maybe I should be going home now," she finished quietly.

"What's this about leaving?" Len protested. "I was looking forward to a game of tennis. You did say you were pretty good, didn't you? I expected you to prove it."

Amber laughed, and the awkward moment passed. "You're on!"

≥≥

Later, at home, Amber reflected on the evening. Her winning game with Len. Their relaxed conversation, the easy camaraderie. The amazing revelation about Layla, the poor, lost daughter. . .though there was much more to that story. Amber was sure of it.

Another part of the conversation came back to her now. She hadn't planned to replay that little scenario, but the thoughts came anyway. If Anton had loved Layla, how could she have asked for anything more?

And what about Anton? Did he still think of Layla, still miss her? He had told Amber that his mother had taught him that, no matter what, life goes on. Did he really believe that? Or, without his mother and Layla, was he merely. . .existing?

ten

On Tuesday Anton called to report that Gina had signed a contract with the shampoo firm. She would be posing for a magazine layout and four television commercials. Therefore, she'd remain in New York for the shoot, while he returned to the office the following week.

Amber wondered what Anton would say when he learned what his secretary had done in his absence. Len had cajoled her into posing for glamour shots, wearing his eye makeup. "Your eyes are perfect for my line," he'd insisted.

"Come on, dear. Humor him," Charis had added with a pleading note in her voice.

The pair had proved an irresistable combination. So she'd given in.

❧

"Do you have plans for the weekend?" Charis asked Amber on Friday afternoon.

"Nothing pressing." She certainly wouldn't turn down an invitation for another evening with her new friends. Besides, she was on a roll in tennis. She'd won her last game with Len six-love.

"Good. I'm having a small dinner party at my house. Anton will be back, you know. And he vows he prefers my home cooking to any of those marvelous restaurants in New York." Charis laughed. "I think it's the atmosphere he likes. He knows he can relax with us."

Amber stifled a groan. *Well,* I *can't. . .not if Anton is there!* But it was too late to back out. She had already admitted that she had no plans.

"Come early so we can play some tennis. Anton enjoys the sport as much as Len."

Friday evening and all morning on Saturday, Amber was a basket case. How many other guests were the Lamarrs expecting? Who would be Anton's date? Gina, of course, was not available. The shoot would take at least a couple of weeks. But Amber was pretty sure her boss would not be lonely long.

She bought a new white tennis outfit to complement her deepening tan, grateful that her skin hadn't burned in the dazzling rays. Then she was furious at herself for caring how she looked!

On Saturday afternoon, Amber parked her blue Escort beside Anton's big Mercedes in the Lamarr driveway, and jumped out. By now she had learned that she could usually find Len and Charis on the terrace, so she walked around to the back of the house. All three, the Lamarrs and Anton, were sitting at an umbrella-shaded table, sipping tall drinks. There was no sign of anyone else. Had Anton come alone? Maybe his dinner guest would join them later.

"Here's my favorite tennis partner now!" Len called, springing to his feet. Charis gestured her toward a lounge chair near Anton.

"Hello, Amber." Anton's dark eyes swept her casual outfit—slacks, shirt, sandals. "That looks like a real California tan. You must have followed the boss's orders."

Ignoring his remark, she dropped into the seat Charis had pointed out. "I trust your trip was successful."

"*Very*. . .thanks to my efficient secretary. I followed your schedule, Amber, and everything went off like clockwork. And I see you've taken my advice and spent some time off in the sun."

When she still didn't answer, Charis spoke up. "No, Anton. She didn't."

He drew his brows together in a mock scowl. "Insubordination will not be tolerated at Pasetti Enterprises, young lady."

In the wake of the laughter that followed, Amber protested mildly, "I didn't need a day off. I relaxed on the weekend." Her mouth was strangely dry, and she was grateful for the iced lemonade Len set before her.

"You mean Charis isn't the slave driver I am?" Anton teased.

"Your secretary is full of insults today, Anton," Len interrupted, pretending to be hurt. "She calls beating me in tennis *relaxation*. Believe me, it was anything *but*."

"Perhaps we can turn the tables on her," Anton said. He finished his drink, set the glass down, and stood. "Are you game?"

She glanced at the two men. They were enjoying this far too much. "No fair for the two of you to gang up on me!"

Charis laughed. "I think I could make it even. Let's chance it. I hope you brought a change."

"Of course. . .just like you taught me. . .but what about dinner? Is there anything I can do?"

"Not a thing. Tillie has everything under control in the kitchen. Now, run get your things and you can use one of our guest rooms."

Amber retrieved the small case she had packed and followed Charis into the house. On the way down the hall, she couldn't resist asking, "When will the others be arriving?"

"Others?" Charis turned a quizzical look on her. "Oh, there will be no other guests. Just the four of us."

Amber had begun to suspect as much. What must Anton think? That she had asked the Lamarrs to set this up?

On the court, Amber's hands felt clammy, her knees shaky. "I don't think this is going to be my day," she confided to Charis.

"Don't worry about it. It's only a game."

Only a game, she thought. *The way some people play games. . . .*

The speeding ball, the quick strokes, the pauses before serves—all passed by in a blur to Amber. She bit her lower lip for better concentration. She could see that Anton was enjoying himself immensely as he moved back and forth across the court in smooth, muscular strides.

It was an easy win for the men.

"Don't think that lets you off the hook, Amber," Len said on the way back to the house. "I'm still determined to beat you in singles. Today's win I have to attribute to Anton."

"I might have had something to do with our losing, too," Charis noted lightly. "But there's always another day. Right, Amber?"

Now that the set was over, Amber felt herself relaxing. "The two of us will have to practice so we can beat them in doubles next time." She shrugged aside the worrisome thought that it was no fun living as a single in a doubles world, then excused herself to freshen up.

After a quick shower, Amber slipped into the mint green dinner dress she had brought, smoothing the full skirt. Studying her reflection in the bathroom mirror, she touched the bodice that dipped to a V in front. Long sleeves of the soft material buttoned at the wrist. Matching green sandals completed the outfit.

After applying fresh makeup, she brushed her hair, grateful for the cut and natural wave as the shining strands fell softly below her shoulders. The sun had brought out golden highlights, she observed approvingly.

When she looked into the mirror for a final inspection, she realized that she barely resembled the same young woman who had fled to California over four months ago. She was almost. . .beautiful. Inside, too, she seemed to be changing. But she wasn't sure it was for the better. The guilt was almost gone. But she was still unsure of herself. Was she hoping that Anton would echo what the mirror was telling her?

Don't be silly, Amber, she chided herself. *You're too sensible. . .too cool and competent for that kind of nonsense.*

Leaving her apprehension behind, she went into the kitchen where Charis had promised to show her a few gourmet cooking tips.

"Mmmm. What is that aroma?" Anton asked, sticking his head around the door.

"Out!" Charis ordered, aiming her spatula at him. "Amber and I can handle this."

"Not until you tell me what it is."

"Poulet à l'estragon."

"Ah, chicken," he translated, to Amber's great relief. "Okay, okay, I'm going," he promised, holding up both hands to ward off Charis's mock blows as he backed out of the kitchen.

"Chicken?" Amber had to laugh in spite of herself. "I'm afraid my French isn't very good."

"Casserole-roasted with tarragon," Charis explained. "First, it's trussed, then browned in butter and oil and roasted in a covered casserole with herbs and seasonings."

"You've never eaten anything so tender," Tillie put in.

The three put the finishing touches to the broiled tomatoes, green peas, stuffed mushrooms, and *pommes dauphines.*

"French potato puffs," Charis translated at Amber's raised eyebrows. "Now, since Tillie doesn't like too many hands in *her* kitchen," she said, untying her apron and laying it aside, "let's go find the men so she can serve dinner."

In the informal dining room, Charis and Amber filled Anton in on office news and learned some of the details about the shampoo deal. Even though it was more painful than Amber wanted to admit to imagine her boss and Gina in that romantic setting, it did feel good to be included in the inner loop of agency talk.

After dessert, coffee was served in the sitting room.

Anton leaned back in a lounge chair and stretched out his long legs. "It's good to be back. Coming here is like coming home, Charis."

"It's home any time you want it to be, Anton. You know that. You're like the son we never had."

If Layla had lived, Anton might have become their son-in-law, Amber thought with a jolt, and wondered if she had read their thoughts. Her cup rattled against the saucer as she placed it on the table beside her chair.

Just then, Len rose to his feet. "There's something I want you to see. Be right back."

Rather than subject herself to Anton's disturbing gaze,

Amber walked over to an open window, allowing the night air to cool her face. She remained there until Len returned. He switched on fluorescent lighting set into the ceiling, and the room was flooded with brilliance.

After placing a leather-bound portfolio on the coffee table, he flipped it open. "Come take a look, Amber," he said, patting the cushion beside him. She obeyed.

"You, too, Anton." Charis motioned to the spot on the other side of her husband. "You'll want to see these."

Amber recognized the photographs instantly. She had posed for those pictures, albeit reluctantly. Now she wondered how Anton would view them.

He took his time, studying each one intently. "This would be one of our models, of course. But there's something else, about the expression. . . ." He leaned forward to inspect the pictures more closely as his voice trailed off. Looking up, he quirked a brow, glancing past Len to Amber. "But this model has. . .brown eyes."

Len turned the page to a full-face photo of Amber. She held her breath, waiting for his reaction.

When it came, it wasn't the explosion she had expected. It was worse. "I. . .see," was all he would say.

"It was just a joke," she put in uncertainly, suddenly feeling like the victim of some conspiracy.

"Oh, it's no joke," Len told her seriously. "You're a natural for the 'haunting' look we're trying to project for our new campaign."

" 'Haunting'?" she croaked, and cleared her throat. "As in 'ghostly'?" Her attempt to lighten the atmosphere failed miserably.

" 'Wistful,' then. There's a certain sadness in your eyes,

Amber." She could see that Len was dead serious now as he turned to Anton. "Can't you see it? It's dynamite! There's a whole story behind that look. And it'll sell, or I have no business trying to pitch beauty products!"

Aware that Len was about to stumble onto her secret, Amber changed the subject. "Have you always worked in the cosmetic industry?"

"No," he replied slowly, "not always."

"I know. I'll bet you were a tennis pro."

"No, my dear." Len closed the portfolio. "I was a psychiatrist. It was my wife who was in the beauty business." He glanced over at Charis, his voice strained. "Oh, I dabbled in a few projects, but I joined her only when it became clear that. . .well, let's just say I was much like the shoemaker whose family went barefoot."

A somber silence settled over the group. No doubt he was referring to Layla, the beloved daughter. Amber found herself wondering again what had caused her death. An accident. . .like Ken's?

Amber stood and walked over to the window. From here, she could barely make out the shoreline, where a choppy sea sent waves crashing against the beach. Even in the near darkness, she could see the foam spewing into the air. Ugly dark clouds scudded angrily across the sky. When had the weather changed? Well, whenever, it mirrored the storm brewing in her soul.

Feeling a masculine touch, she jumped. But it was only Len's arm around her shoulders. "Now I'm in the beauty business full-time, and dabble in tennis with lovely young women on the side," he said, his old self again. "And one of these days, I'm going to beat you in singles!"

"Promises, promises!" She gave him an affectionate pat. "But it'll have to wait for another day." Out of the corner of her eye, she saw that Anton had drifted off into a world of his own. "Thanks for a lovely evening."

Anton got to his feet when he saw that she was about to leave. "I'll walk you to the car."

Outside, jagged streaks of lightning split the sky. But there was no rain. And there was no conversation on the way to the car, either. Instead, a sullen silence fell between them.

When they reached the car, Anton barred her way by leaning against her door. Amber had no choice but to halt in front of him. The expression in his eyes was veiled, even in the half-light, but his face looked grim and stormy.

Of course! The photographs! But surely he wasn't taking them seriously. She had only agreed to pose to end Len's pleading.

"I hope you understand that those photos weren't my idea," she said with a trace of embarrassment.

"Len is a client," Anton stated flatly. "He apparently wants you to advertise his product. Unless you refuse or he changes his mind, that's how it will be."

"But if you. . .disapprove—" she began, and stuttered to a stop at the look of contempt on his face.

"That's my business, remember?"

"But I'm a secretary, not a model."

"Try telling that to Len."

"He also thinks I'm a tennis pro."

He shrugged. "As long as you're posing for photographs and winning matches, then I suppose you qualify," he snapped.

Funny. She had noticed a softening toward him in the

few days before he left for New York. Now, just as she had begun to care for him, she felt she didn't know him at all. It shouldn't matter what Anton Pasetti thought, but for some reason she wanted him to believe that she was not serious about modeling.

"I'm your secretary *first*. Any other. . .project. . .would be temporary." She watched, but his stern expression didn't change. "Tonight. . .in there. . .you seemed—"

"Surprised?" he finished for her. "Believe me, I wasn't surprised to find out you'd agreed to pose for Len." The muscle in his jaw clenched. "It was just that the expression in the eyes reminded me of someone else." Silhouetted against the threatening sky, he towered over her like the stormy hero in some gothic novel. "The critics said she had the most photogenic eyes they had ever seen."

Layla! The truth dawned on Amber just as a crash of thunder sounded overhead. That was it! That was why Len and Charis had taken her in and treated her like their own daughter. Why even Anton had appeared drawn to her.

"I have to go," she said, feeling any explanation she might give would fall on deaf ears.

He reached for the door handle and opened the door. She slid behind the wheel, while he bent down to speak through the open window. "Just think of the publicity." His tone was laced with sarcasm. "I can see the headlines now: 'From Memos to Model Overnight!' Only you and I know it wasn't 'overnight,' don't we. . .*Miss Jennings?*" he flung at her. "You didn't waste any time, did you? You took advantage of my first business trip!"

The verbal assault felt like a physical blow. He believed she had deliberately set out to do this, had insinuated it all along. Amber clenched the steering wheel. She must not let him intimidate her. "I do *not* want to be a model!" she insisted. "I refuse to be."

"Oh? You're *full* of surprises, aren't you?"

"Anton Pasetti, sometimes I despise you! So go ahead and fire me now!" She plunged the key into the ignition and started the engine. It sprang to life.

"Fire you?" He spat out the words. "That would only make it easier for you to pursue another career—probably with a competitor! And don't tell me you wouldn't! Or that anyone taking *one* look at you wouldn't hire you on the spot!"

The wash of joy that flooded her ebbed at his next words. "What you didn't have in the beginning. . .Pasetti Agency *gave* you!"

She was quite aware that she had begun to desire his compliments, to need them as much as a thirsty flower needs rain. Now all she wanted was to hurt him as he had hurt her. "You can't bear to think you might be wrong about a person, can you? That every female who comes into your office is only interested in becoming a model. . .or," she forced the words past her aching throat, "or in *you!*"

He seemed momentarily taken aback, then shrugged. "Regardless of what you think of me, the Lamarr deal would be profitable all the way around. I'd suggest you consider it, Miss Jennings. Besides, since the agency has taught you to make the most of your beauty, surely you realize the obligation on your part."

"No!" she retorted, hating his placid manner, hating most of all his distrust of her. "I earn my paycheck. I don't owe you anything more. Why can't you just let me do my job. . .and leave me alone?" She gunned the engine, ready to spin off.

But something in his expression held her. "Secretaries can be replaced," he called over the roar of another crash of thunder, "but how many beautiful women could give Len Lamarr the pleasure of launching the career his own daughter missed? Since you've gone this far, Amber, could you refuse him now?"

She couldn't take any more of this. She pulled away, her tears blinding her just as heavy drops of rain splatted against the windshield. Switching on the wiper, she dashed away the tears with one hand. In the rear-view mirror she could see Anton standing where she had left him in the sudden downpour.

On the way home, she calmed down enough to think more clearly. It was easy to see why he didn't trust her, she had to admit. It *did* look pretty suspicious, as if she'd wangled her way into Len's life to gain his approval. And she *had* consented to the photo session, though she hadn't expected anything to come of it.

Now it was too late. Anton obviously felt she was obligated to follow through, but he would never again trust her, never believe that she was. . .different. . .from other women.

The few times she'd tried to share her testimony with Anton were now worthless. Somehow she had to prove to Anton that she was telling the truth about her motives, her goals, her faith in God. But she couldn't help but wonder if even God Himself could undo the mess she'd made of things.

eleven

In the next few days, the office was a zoo. Anton had to be briefed on what had taken place during his absence, and follow-ups had to be made on his business contacts in New York.

For Amber, the worst part of her job all week was to type in her own name on the contract for Lamarr Cosmetics.

Her gaze kept turning to Gina's photograph on the wall of the office. Gina had modeled for the line last year, and Amber felt those green eyes flashing her a warning not to sign. Actually, she had no intention of signing the contract. Still, she was expected to draw it up, along with others, for Anton's Thursday night dinner date with Len.

After lunch in the cafeteria on Wednesday, Amber was back at her desk when Anton stopped by. He was holding a leather tote bag in one hand. "Have someone cover for you," he ordered in his most Pasetti-professional tone. "I want you to go with me."

She called Charis for a replacement, then got her purse and emergency makeup kit from the bottom desk drawer and followed him out the door.

Without another word, he took her arm and steered her toward the elevator. All the way to the first floor, he didn't break the silence. Amber figured there was an important meeting with some client. Must be a difficult one, too, judging from that stony expression. On the other hand, he wasn't carrying his briefcase.

In the parking lot, he opened the car door for her. "Hold onto this," he said, tossing the bag into her lap.

He walked around to the driver's side, slid behind the wheel, and started the car.

On the freeway, he sent several curious glances in her direction. "Aren't you going to ask where we're going?"

Amber shrugged. "I assumed you'd tell me eventually," she replied coldly, keeping her eyes straight ahead.

Just as suddenly as the sun breaking through dark clouds after the rain, his manner changed. "It's a lovely day. Much too nice to be cooped up in an office, don't you agree?"

Now her suspicions were aroused, and she couldn't resist asking, "Where *are* we going?"

"Does it matter?"

"I like to be prepared."

"You will be." He laughed, nodding toward the tote bag in her lap. "Take a look."

Amber opened the bag and pulled out a brown-and-white checked, two-piece swimsuit. It looked like something Gina would wear. But Gina was still in New York. Feeling around in the bottom of the bag, she found a white terry beach wrap, trimmed in brown. "We're going to a photographic session at the beach." No doubt they would be meeting the model at their destination.

"Partly right." He smiled a secretive smile.

"We're going to a photographic session. . .but *not* at the beach."

"Try it the other way around." He turned off the freeway onto a familiar exit.

Silently, she returned the swimwear to the bag. No need to ask any more questions. She knew where they were going. Instead, she looked out the window while Anton made the expected turns, moving relentlessly toward his beachside estate.

When they arrived, she made no effort to get out of the car but waited for him to walk around and open the door. He stood, waiting while she stepped out. . .dragging her feet.

"Come now, Amber," he said in a smooth voice, "must you look so stricken?" A quick gleam lighted his eyes and his lips tilted slightly upward.

She refused to give him the satisfaction of thinking she could be charmed by his congenial manner, as if they were off simply to enjoy an afternoon together. There was some devious motive lurking behind his actions, and she would be on guard every single minute!

He sighed. "Come along. There's something we need to discuss in the library."

She trudged silently beside him, begrudging every step, hearing the echo of their feet against the tiles. He opened the wrought-iron gate, and she walked onto the back patio. It was much as she remembered it, only more spacious and without all the picnic guests.

When they got to the library, Anton motioned her to the couch, while he drew up a chair nearby. "Do you remember that, before I left for New York, I ordered you to take a day off?"

She glared at him. "You don't have any right to tell me what to do—or *not* to do—with my free time. I took that as a *suggestion.*"

"Well, I'm here to see that you take me up on my. . . suggestion. I'm giving you an afternoon free of responsibility. I want you to enjoy yourself here. . .as a gesture of my appreciation for your conscientious work."

"That's completely unnecessary," she retorted. "My salary is ample compensation for what I do for you."

He ignored the remark. "Feel free to use the pool or the beach. . .or simply relax here with a good book." With a wave of his hand, he indicated the floor-to-ceiling library of leather-bound volumes. "If you need me, a servant will know where to find me."

He got to his feet and was about to leave when something seemed to occur to him. "Oh, yes, there's something else." He drew out some familiar-looking papers from the inner pocket of his suit coat, unfolded them, and laid them on the table. "Give this some thought this afternoon. I'll be taking the contract to Len this evening. There's a pen on the desk."

With that, he turned abruptly and left the room.

So *that* was why he had brought her here! He expected her to sign Len's contract. What was he up to, anyway? One minute he was accusing her of having ulterior motives about modeling; the next, he was practically demanding she sign on the dotted line!

A tap on the door intruded on her thoughts. Maybe Anton had forgotten something. "Yes?"

It was a maid, bringing lemonade and light refreshments. Even the house staff was well-trained, Amber thought, certain she wasn't the first woman he had brought here under false pretenses. Probably all the servants were accustomed to Anton's romantic escapades. Not that *she* was his most recent conquest. That would be *Gina!*

Suddenly realizing that she was a prisoner in this isolated place, Amber felt a sense of panic. She had to get out of here! But she had no car, no way to get back to the cottage.

The maid was still in the room, arranging sandwiches on a plate.

"Please," Amber began, "could you tell me how to find the bell tower?" Maybe from there, she could see a way out. At least she might be able to think more clearly. Anton had told her that when he needed relief from his mother's suffering, he'd often gone there.

"Yes, ma'am. The tower room is always unlocked. My husband, Mitchell, sees to that. Just go up one floor and take the stairs at the end of the hall. That will lead you to the tower. There's a beautiful view from those windows."

So Mitchell was her husband. Amber thought she had detected a glimmer of curiosity in the woman's glance. No doubt Mr. Mitchell had overseen the episode with Anton on the beach after the picnic and had told his wife about it. Feeling her cheeks flush, Amber thanked her and hurried from the room, absent-mindedly carrying the tote bag with her.

The bell tower wasn't difficult to find. As Mrs. Mitchell had said, it was right at the top of the second flight of stairs.

Amber creaked open the heavy door and found a small, squarish room, bounded on three sides with benches, a huge bell suspended from the ceiling. The large clapper would undoubtedly make a sound that could be heard for miles. She resisted the urge to ring it.

In each of the three walls was an arched opening. To the right, a tree-studded area stretched as far as the eye could see; through the arch directly in front of her, was a view of the formal gardens at the back, the pool, and tennis court. To the left, in the distance, shimmering under the mid-afternoon sun, was the ocean, the rays of light glancing off the waves like small explosions.

She thought of Anton, wondering if he had found the peace he'd been seeking here. . .or out there, on the beach. No doubt his mother had hoped that in this place of solitude, with the evidence of God's creative work all around him, her son would turn to the Lord for comfort. Poor woman. She had died, with her prayers unanswered. Amber felt pity and pain tearing at her, then a surge of anger at the man who left nothing but misery in his wake.

She stared at the vast expanse of water across the rocky shoreline. It drew her like a magnet. Strangely, she didn't fear the ocean as she did the lake that had claimed her parents' lives. A swim would do her good. Maybe on the beach, with the sound of the surf blocking out all the angry words she and Anton had exchanged, she could hear the Lord telling her what to do—about the contract, about Anton, about her life.

She left the tower and found Mrs. Mitchell on the way down. "I think I spotted Mr. Pasetti's private beach from the bell tower. It looked so lovely and peaceful, I'd like to go for a swim. But I'm not sure how to get there."

"It's through the gardens, ma'am, past the pool and tennis court to the left. You'll see it. But watch the steps going down from the terrace. They can be dangerous."

In one of the guest rooms, Amber changed into the swimsuit Anton had brought for her. It was not exactly the type of suit she would choose. Good thing he'd never see her in it. She wrapped the cover-up securely around her, then headed for the beach.

The steps Mrs. Mitchell had mentioned were steep and narrow, and Amber was careful making her way down. At the bottom, she realized that the beach was actually a cove, walled in by perpendicular cliffs. Stretching to the far horizon was the ocean, silver-tipped waves swelling toward the shore. She stood for a moment, drinking in the stillness. Only the cry of a gull and the rhythmic ebb and flow of the waves against the coastline disturbed the serenity. It was a pocket of peace in the midst of all the confusion of the past few days.

She breathed in deeply, feeling the tension in her muscles beginning to ease. A stiff sea breeze tugged playfully at her beach wrap as if daring her to feel the kiss of the sun on her skin. She loosed the ties and dropped the cover-up onto the rocky beach.

Running to the water's edge, she exulted in the sensation of wind-whipped hair, glad she hadn't tied it back. It was glorious! Wind in her face—like the brush of angels' wings—and warm sand beneath her feet. *Thank You, Lord,* she breathed, loosing her cares as easily as she had shed the cover-up. *I know You have the answers. Just give me the patience I need.*

She dashed into the water—not as icy as the mountain streams back home but brisk and invigorating. With her face tilted toward the rain-washed sky, brilliantly blue and almost an ache to the eyes, she missed seeing a huge swell rolling toward shore. Before she knew what had hit her, she was knocked off balance and pulled under by a strong current. Struggling to find her footing, she came up gasping and choking, sea water streaming from her drenched hair.

From the beach, the sound of masculine laughter brought an aftershock. Anton!

"When you run headlong into the ocean, don't expect to win!" he called, still laughing. "And watch out for the undertow. It's strong this time of the afternoon."

"How. . .how long have you been standing there?" she sputtered, accepting his hand as he waded out to lead her to shore. "Long enough. This *is* my private beach, you know. . .my retreat from the rat race." He offered her a towel. She grabbed it gratefully and covered herself, rubbing vigorously to shake the chill. "You're one of very few who have ever been here."

"Oh. . .I'm sorry. No one told me I shouldn't—"

He stopped her with an uplifted hand. "Now that you *are*," he leaned over to pick up the cover-up she had dropped on the beach, "maybe we'd better protect that skin. Models have to be especially careful in the sun."

Hurriedly she finished blotting herself dry and slipped into the wrap, fastening it securely around her waist. "I'm not a model."

"You didn't sign?"

"No."

There was a stony silence between them, with only the sound of the surf and a sea bird or two calling to each other above the cliffs.

His jaw flexed. "Well, we can't stand here." He eyed

the water rising to fill half the beach. "The tide will get us soon." The tide was advancing rapidly, making pools in the rocky indentations before rolling back out to sea.

He strode over to an area against the cliffs where he had only recently been sitting, she guessed. She followed reluctantly.

He turned to face her, his expression grim. "I suppose you know that Gina will be offered the contract if you refuse to sign."

Amber nodded, acutely conscious of her bedraggled appearance—hair slicked back, face washed clean of makeup. Even here, in this deserted place, she couldn't escape the flawless image of the beautiful redhead.

"She's flying in tonight from New York. Her contract with Len is up for renewal. Tomorrow she expects to be told whether Len wants her for the new campaign, or whether he's signed. . .a new model."

Amber lifted her chin. "Then tell her the contract is hers. I made my decision before you brought me here." She could feel the sparks shooting from her eyes.

For a moment, he didn't respond. Then a slow grin split his face. He looked ridiculously boyish. "You're irresistible when you're angry, you know." His expression shifted, and something unfamiliar flickered in his eyes.

His words were charged with tension when he spoke again. "You may not be a model. And today you're not a secretary. But you *are*. . .a very desirable woman."

She was suddenly aware of his nearness—the massive shoulders, the bare chest, the strong jawline. She could not look away. A storm of emotion swirled inside her. Like the strong ocean currents, she felt herself drawn into the undertow. She was helpless. . .powerless.

Amost against his will, it seemed, Anton backed away. "But then. . .Ken, is it? is the one true love of your life . . .and you've never gotten over him."

Amber's breath caught in her throat. How could she answer him without exposing her newly discovered feelings?

Anton shrugged. "You're suspicious of me—not without justification, I must admit—but I do know the honorable thing to do." He quirked a brow. "You're either a true innocent, or you're playing a very convincing game. And not even *I* can decide which it is."

"I don't play games, Mr. Pasetti. I've told you before." The shadows loomed darker as the sun sank toward the sea. How could she be so ambivalent—despising him one minute, wanting him to crush her in his arms the next?

He narrowed his gaze. "Oh, I think you may be playing the most dangerous game of your life. Gina says you're determined to be more than my secretary." He cocked his head as if trying to gauge the effects of his next words. "She thinks you want to be. . .my *wife*."

Amber exploded in a volley of words. "How could she say something like that? I've never done anything to make her think. . .and why would I want to be your wife? I don't even *like* you, Mr. Pasetti! You're arrogant, egotistical. . .and cruel!" Shaken to the core, Amber turned and ran across the rocky beach, now covered with water.

His laughter mocked her, ricocheting off the cliffsides. "And don't forget. . .immoral and godless!"

A wall as hard and impenetrable as the rock walls fell between them. Her tears blinded her, and she hurried toward the narrow steps. How could things have gotten so out of control? Even God seemed as remote as this secluded cove.

Finding the path, she rushed up, her bare feet slapping against the slippery wooden steps. She was out of breath, as much from anger and frustration as from exertion. The man was maddening! If she never saw him again, it would be too soon! Just a few more steps. . . .

Her last thought was of Anton before she lost her footing and felt herself falling.

twelve

Gina swept into the office, red hair flaming like fire in a shaft of sunlight pouring in through the reception room window. "Is Anton alone?"

Amber looked up. "I'll buzz."

The woman's green eyes were coolly calculating today. "Don't bother. After all the time we spent together in New York. . . ."

The implication was clear. But in the next minute, as Amber turned her head to press the intercom button, Gina gasped. "What happened to you? You look *awful!*"

Automatically Amber reached up to touch the tender flesh under her right eye. She winced. It was still swollen and horribly black and blue, despite her efforts to camouflage it with makeup this morning. "Oh. . .it's nothing. Just ran into . . .a little problem." Gina was the *last* person she'd tell how she'd ended up with the world's biggest shiner!

"Well, whatever it was, you sure got the worst end of the deal. Too bad." Gina flounced past the desk on her way into Anton's office, throwing Amber a smile that was more condescending than concerned.

Amber flinched when the door clicked shut behind the woman. Her headache was only slightly worse than the ache in her heart. Already Gina would be gloating. Probably she was in Anton's arms right now, celebrating her triumph.

After what had happened at his house last night. . . .

Amber recalled her nasty spill down the cliffside steps, hitting her head on the way down. How humiliating that, after the stormy scene with Anton on the beach, she'd ended up sprawling at the bottom of the steps at his feet! But when he'd helped her up and checked her over for serious injury, there had been only the one spot, reddening around her eye.

"The angels caught you," Aunt Sophie would have said. Amber believed it. How else could she have escaped such a fall with nothing more than a black eye?

She was pretty sure that Anton was counting his blessings, too. Good thing for him she hadn't signed that contract for Len's line of eye makeup. Now Gina would have clear sailing.

Amber was pouring herself a second cup of coffee when she decided to take a breather. It was about time for her morning break anyway. She'd just ask Charis to send a replacement a little early, then she'd beat a hasty retreat to the older woman's office at the other end of the hall. No need to put herself through the torment of seeing Gina and Anton coming out of his office together—if they ever *did*.

"Come in, dear." Charis didn't look up from some papers on her desk until Amber took a seat, at eye level. "Oh, my! You poor darling!" Charis exclaimed the minute she saw her. "Anton told me about your little accident, but I wasn't prepared to see you looking like the victim of a train wreck."

Amber gave a wry grin, then grimaced in pain. "I know I'm a mess. But it could have been a lot worse."

"Have you been putting ice packs on that eye?" Charis rose to come around her desk.

"That. . .and beefsteak, too. Mitchell and his wife, Edna, couldn't have been nicer. Anton even insisted on calling in a doctor. But I'm fine. . .really. No broken bones. Only *this* monster."

Charis took Amber's face in one hand, tilting her head to study the injury. "What a shame. But there's no real damage done. Nothing that a little more concealer couldn't fix."

"Oh, I'm not worried. The doctor said it would be as good as new in a couple of weeks. It's just that. . . ."

Charis leaned back against her desk, arms folded over her chest. She looked regal today in royal blue, Amber thought, like a queen. "Yes, Amber?"

She resisted the urge to let the whole ugly truth spill out. Her lack of love for Ken, who was the right kind of man for her. Her disturbing feelings for Anton, who was anything *but* right for her. Her—yes, she might as well admit it, if only to herself—her jealousy of Gina's hold over him. And now, even if she wanted to sign Len's contract. . . .

Like the surf rushing over the rocky shore and washing back to sea, she let her thoughts ebb away.

"Well, if you haven't anything to tell *me*," Charis began, "I have something to tell *you*."

Amber jerked to attention.

"We really want you to reconsider Len's offer, dear."

Amber was stunned. Charis couldn't mean what she was saying. Not with this face looking like something out of a horror movie!

"There's more to it than the eye makeup line alone." Charis rose once more, her silk dress rustling as she moved over to a window and looked out over the city skyline. "A colleague. . .in the clothing business. . .has seen your photographs, thinks you have the wholesome, innocent look she needs for a new line and wants you for a fashion spread. . .in Paris."

Amber was barely able to catch her breath. Paris! The ultimate escape. A place to lose her memories, to find herself. Was this the answer to her prayers? "Paris? But my job. . .my eye—"

Charis turned to face her. "Anton is willing to release you for the project. The two shoots won't take more than a month at most, and Len could design his campaign around the Paris theme. As for your eye. . . ." She cocked her head and gave a mysterious little smile. "Do you remember the old movies starring a blond by the name of Veronica Lake? Her signature hairstyle was a side part, with hair swinging forward to cover. . .the right side of her face."

Amber was still speechless, though her mind was whirring with the speed of a Pentium 133. Maybe she could get away long enough to forget Anton Pasetti.

"And there's always Len's great cosmetics," Charis was saying. "He carries the best concealer in the business, you know."

Concealer. . . . The truth burst on Amber with all the intensity of the San Diego sunshine. Secrets. . .Ken. . . she owed it to Charis to tell her about that episode in her life—even if she was as confused as ever about Anton. "Before you decide whether or not you really want me for this assignment, there's something I have to say."

❧

On the way to lunch, there were murmurs of sympathy

from practically everyone in the building. Even the women who had hated Amber for outdoing them in her Mexican outfit, were now coming up to offer their condolences. And why not? With this eye, she was no threat to anyone!

It was only after Ron fixed her up with a black patch that made her look like a gun moll or a female buccaneer that the women began to ignore her again.

"They can't *stand* it when someone else takes the limelight," Kate muttered, moving through the line. "You'd think they'd be happy you weren't *killed* in that fall!" She frowned at a group leaving the cafeteria, no doubt talking about Amber. "Uh, oh! Don't look now, but here comes Miss You-Know-Who."

Amber couldn't resist.

"Hi, you two," Gina said brightly. "Mind if I join you?" Not waiting for a reply, she set her tray down. Removing her birdlike meal from the tray, she placed it on the table and sat. "How can you girls eat that fatty food?" she asked, wrinkling her nose.

"People who work hard need the energy," Kate snapped.

"Work?" Gina scoffed. "You don't know what work is! Try sitting under hot lights with the cameras grinding away. Try having your hair shampooed half a dozen times a day."

Amber continued munching on her chicken salad sandwich.

"But," Gina added in a snide tone, "I suppose Amber will soon learn. . .now that she's a model."

So Anton had told her, Amber thought. *Wonder if he knows why I signed that contract. . .that I can't take being in the same office with him. . .that I'm tempted to love him when I know I can never have him.* . . . "I'm not a model yet, Gina. In the meantime, I'm still a secretary."

"Lamarr Cosmetics doesn't think so. Anton doesn't think so." Gina was breathing hard. "And a signed contract, the one Charis's other little secretary delivered while I was in his office, says otherwise!"

Amber stiffened. She didn't want to tangle with Gina over this. "Look, Len had those photos taken on a whim. I'm no model and I don't want to be."

"Ha! As if you didn't worm your way into landing that contract behind my back, while I was in New York!"

"Oh, come off it, Gina," Kate put in defensively. "Can't you be satisfied with the shampoo commercials? There's enough to go around in this business."

Gina shot her a withering look.

"Just a minute." Amber held up a hand. "I didn't ask for the contract. Just what are you talking about?"

"Oh, Anton told me all about it. How you've been cozying up to the Lamarrs. . .playing tennis with Len, seeing him in his home. Said Len was intrigued with a certain air about you. . .like you're hiding some deep, dark secret that's just perfect for his new campaign." She stabbed a piece of lettuce with her fork. "What *I* think you're hiding is your scheming and conniving to get what you want!"

Kate came up out of her seat, eyes flashing. "That's not true!"

"Oh, really?" Gina returned her scorching look. "Well now, how would it seem to you if you went away with your boss and heard nothing but talk of his 'dedicated, efficient little secretary,' who was grieving her little heart out over a lost fiancé—and then came home to find out that not only had she taken your *job* but she was trying to take your *man!*"

"Of all the rotten things to say!" Kate began. "Amber is not like that at all. *You're* the one who would stoop to anything to get what you want!"

Amber moaned.

Gina arched a well-groomed brow. "I know a few tricks . . .but your little friend here *uses* them. She used her grief to play on Len's and Anton's sympathy, for one thing." She darted an appraising glance at Amber. "Frankly, I don't think you're suffering at all."

Suddenly Amber had had enough of being sweet and patient. "Listen, you. . .you don't know the meaning of love or grief, because you don't *have* a heart! I *did* grieve for Ken and I loved him, though not as much as he wanted or deserved." Amber rushed on, her volume increasing. "I wore the engagement ring out of respect. But I've put the whole sad thing behind me. What's wrong with that? Why should you assume I'm putting on some—" She broke off, horrified to see Anton coming into the cafeteria.

Gina did not miss the direction of her gaze. "So you say you don't play games? I know the truth. You want Anton for yourself, don't you?"

"I don't have to stay here and listen to this!" Amber grabbed her purse and, leaving her half-eaten lunch on the table, rushed from the cafeteria, Gina's mocking laughter trailing her all the way out the door.

❧

Anton paused at the threshold of the reception room door,

eyes wide. Amber had never seen him shaken—except maybe at that moment at the bottom of the steps when he'd thought she might be seriously injured—or dead! Now he seemed able only to stare before walking slowly past her desk, his eyes riveted on her new hairstyle.

After lunch, Amber had fled again to Charis's office in tears to vent her frustration over Gina's latest accusation—although she carefully avoided mentioning that the redhead was on the right track. Amber *was* attracted to Anton, but she was fighting it with everything she had in her. Besides, Layla was still in the picture. . .and a woman couldn't win over the memory of a lost love. Not that she was hoping to win. Oh, she didn't know *what* she was hoping! She only knew she always felt better when she was with Charis.

With the older woman's help, Amber had removed the eyepatch Ron had playfully created out of construction paper. Then, with Charis's help, she'd parted her hair on the left, swept it to one side, and allowed the silky strands to fall over her face. The effect was amazing! The black eye was completely covered, while the lift at her hairline on the left cast the planes of her face in a whole new light. Charis had been delighted. "Just wait until Len sees *this!* His 'Woman of Mystery' campaign will be the hottest thing he's ever done!"

It was only seconds after Anton reached his inner office that he buzzed for Amber. She set her phone to transfer all incoming calls to voice mail, grabbed her laptop, and reported dutifully, taking her usual chair beside his desk.

"You won't need to take notes, Amber."

Her startled glance at him revealed the granitelike mask of his expression. What was this all about? Some glitch in the contract already?

After a moment, he swiveled his chair back, stood, and turned to look out the window. "You'll be leaving for Paris next week. . .for the fashion shoot and the cosmetic lay-out."

So soon? She permitted only a small intake of breath.

"We'll have some details to clear up before you go. Would you. . .go out with me this weekend?" His tone held a dare. . .or was it the first trace of humility she'd ever observed in him?

She didn't know what to say. Was this business or plea-sure? She had no wish to torture herself further. But she would soon be out of here. Maybe this would be her last chance to try to live her Christian witness in front of Anton—after she'd just blown it in the cafeteria. Could she do it? *Lord, help me.*

"Well?" he asked, turning around to face her. As on the day of her interview, the sun was slanting through the win-dow at that peculiar angle that blinded her and cast him in the shadows. "Will you go with me?"

He was probably hoping she'd refuse. . .to prove she had no designs on him. But until the plans were actually finalized for the Paris shoot, she was still his secretary.

"Yes, sir. Of course. What's the occasion?"

He narrowed his gaze curiously. "Celebration of your new career."

She stiffened. So this was to be "personal." "All right," she told him, looking him in the eye. "I'd need to know when and where."

He seemed to be surprised at her answer. "O-of course. Dinner," he said, returning to his chair at the desk. "An elegant place on the ocean front. Quite formal."

"What time?"

"I'll call for you at seven. . .if that would be agreeable with you."

She nodded. It was pretty satisfying to see him groping for words for a change. "I'll be ready."

He rose, still staring at her as if he couldn't believe what he'd just heard. "Then I guess that will be all. . .for now."

Amber stood, shut her laptop, and without another glance his way, left the office. But the minute she was out the door, she was wondering why she'd ever agreed to such a crazy idea!

❧

On Friday afternoon, after she had gathered her belongings at work and left early, Amber laid out her outfit for her dinner date with Anton. At Charis's insistence, she had accepted the loan of a stunning sleeveless, scoop-necked sheath they'd found in Wardrobe. "It's that delicious shade of hot pink that looks so good on you, Amber."

"But the back. . . ." The back dropped away to a deep V, exposing Amber's California tan.

"It's completely modest, dear," Charis had assured her. "Don't worry. We wouldn't let a Pasetti model out in just any old thing—especially not *this* Pasetti model." She had rummaged in a jewelry drawer and come up with a string of faux pearls and matching pearl-and-diamond earrings. A pair of barely-there sandals, studded with glittering stones, completed the ensemble.

Amber felt a hint of panic. What was she doing, going out with a man who had the ability to take her breath and spin her head and her heart every which way but loose? There was much more preparation to be done before she'd be ready to meet Anton Pasetti. And so she prayed.

She prayed in the shower. *Lord, please clean me up on the inside, too. Help me get rid of all the ugly feelings I've had about Gina. And, Lord, keep me pure . . .even in my thoughts about Anton.*

She prayed as she was dressing. *Clothe me in Your beauty, Lord—kindness and gentleness. Help him see You in me. Teach me how to be a friend to this man who needs You so much.*

She prayed as she was drying her hair and brushing it out to camouflage her right eye, now a sickening yellow-green. *Thank You, Lord, for sparing my life that night I fell. I could have broken my neck! Was it for this moment? To share my faith one last time with this bitter, angry man?*

When she was ready, Amber took one final look at herself in the floor-length mirror on the back of the bathroom door. "Not too bad on the outside. At least, that eye doesn't show. I just hope my insides are ready for this."

With a final desperate prayer for guidance, Amber went to answer Anton's knock. *Help, Lord!* The man was devastatingly handsome in his black tux and starched white shirt, a bowtie knotted perfectly at his throat. *Send Your angels to protect me, as You did the other night. But this time, send them to protect me—from myself!*

thirteen

"If anyone ever had the Pasetti look. . . ." For a moment Anton seemed speechless. "In a word, Amber, you're. . . *perfection!*"

His gaze was openly admiring as he took in her evening attire—from the top of her satin-smooth hair, draped over one eye, to the tip of her rhinestone-studded sandals.

She caught her breath, praying that she wouldn't betray her thudding heart. "I might say the same for you, sir."

He quirked a brow. "Sir? Since when have we been so formal after hours?"

"Until I leave for Paris, I believe I'm still your secretary . . .Mr. Pasetti." Amber picked up a light wrap that Charis had found for her, "In case you two take a moonlight stroll on the beach," she had said with a knowing look. "I'm ready."

He took a step forward, arms outstretched. For a moment, she was afraid he meant to take her in his arms. But something in her one uncovered eye held him at bay. He stared hypnotically, then backed away. "There's something. . .different. . .about you tonight," he mumbled under his breath. "I'm not quite sure—"

"The new hairdo," she supplied.

He shook his head wonderingly.

"The outfit then? Incidentally, it's straight out of Pasetti Wardrobe. Charis—"

"Keep it. It's exactly right for you. . .but, no. . . ." He shook off whatever seemed to be troubling him, and glanced at his watch. "We'd better be going. Our reservations are for seven."

His touch was restrained as he escorted her through the front door of the little cottage, then taking her keys from her hand, he turned and locked up behind them. He handed her into the front seat of the Mercedes as if he were afraid she might break.

There was little conversation on their way into the city. Anton kept his eyes on the road except for an occasional glance at Amber, that expression of puzzlement still in his eyes.

With the ocean on one side and the moon riding low in the sky on the other, Amber drifted through the night at his side. God was watching over them. Angels hovered around them. She could *feel* the peace. She only wished Anton could feel it, too.

≈

At the restaurant—an upscale beachfront structure with an elegant nautical decor—the maitre d' showed them to a corner table overlooking the ocean. On the way through the crowded room, Amber noticed heads turning and whispered conversation. With his picture often in the society pages of the paper and news of the agency in the business section, Anton Pasetti would be recognizable anywhere.

In the center of the skirted table, tall candles flickered in a crystal candelabra. Overhead, brass chandeliers sparkled with a thousand tiny subdued lights, mirrored in the vast expanse of glass walls and water beyond. An orchestra played music from another era, while well-dressed couples danced to the haunting tunes. It was a scene straight out of one of the slick magazines featuring Pasetti models, she thought. And catching sight of the reflected image of herself and Anton in the window-wall next to their table, she couldn't help feeling that, tonight at least, the two of them could qualify for some cover.

No sooner had they been seated than a waiter appeared. With a flourish, he presented them with oversized menus tasseled in gold.

"Eddie," Anton greeted him. "I see you're back. And how is your mother doing after her surgery?"

"Oh, she's much better, Mr. Pasetti. And she asked me to thank you for. . .well, you know what you did for us." He ducked his head in embarrassment, then seemed to remember his place and spoke up briskly. "And what will you. . . and your dinner guest be having tonight, Mr. Pasetti?" The young man gave Amber a curious glance before stepping aside to wait discreetly while Anton studied the choices.

No doubt he had come here many times before, probably with Gina or some of the other models, Amber guessed. She was thoughtful as she watched the handsome man so intent on making just the right selection. He did everything with such panache. She couldn't help admiring that trait—not to mention his legendary acts of benevolence. He was always doing something nice for someone, usually someone who couldn't afford it—like the waiter's mother.

For a moment she wavered in her resolve to keep her distance. Then she recalled something she'd heard in a sermon once: "Good deeds will not earn the reward of heaven without a personal experience with Jesus Christ." Anton Pasetti was not a believer. He'd said so himself.

She steeled herself against his charm, his human kindness. And when he glanced over the top of the menu with that dazzling smile of his, she was ready for him.

"Please order for me," she said, once more in control of her fickle emotions. "I'm sure I'd enjoy anything you chose. You have exquisite taste."

"Yes. . .I have, haven't I?" His gaze warmed, lingered on her eyes, her hair, her lips. The man got to her, and she very nearly weakened again. How could he affect her so deeply without even so much as a touch? She should never have agreed to come to this romantic place. *Lord, keep me strong!*

She was relieved when he turned to the waiter and handed him the menu. "Then we'll have the crab bisque for starters, Eddie. And the filet mignon with shrimp as our entree."

To avoid further awkward moments, Amber shifted her attention to the moonlit beach, the waves rolling in to caress the shore. Even the elements seemed to be conspiring against her. "Um, the tide is coming in, I see. Does the waterline ever reach the restaurant?" she asked, then blushed. It seemed an inane question.

He shook his head. "Unless there's a storm. . .or in the unlikely event of a tidal wave. Nature seems to know her limits."

Amber wondered if she knew *hers*. A storm was raging within her at this very moment. Allowing herself to be in Anton's company tonight—even if she *would* be safely out of the country by tomorrow—was probably a big mistake. It was one thing to pray for protection from temptation, but quite another to deliberately plant oneself in the middle of it!

She was more than relieved when the food was served and they could turn their attention to the exotic dishes. Since crab was not usually included in her weekly grocery budget, she was prepared to enjoy the experience. She savored each spoonful of the delicate, creamy bisque.

But when Eddie brought in the main course, served on domed silver platters, and he whisked off the covers, Amber gasped. "Oh, Anton, I've never eaten lobster before!" she confessed. "How—"

He chuckled. "Don't worry. The shell is for decoration only. All the work has been done for you."

With her fork, she tested the dish—the meat of the lobster cooked in a rich sauce and stuffed inside the imposing shell— and found it to be flaky and tender, easily removed with a flick of the wrist. She had to giggle. "When you ordered lobster, I figured I'd have to wrestle the thing for my dinner!"

By the end of the meal, she was completely relaxed— for the first time since leaving the cottage. Dessert was *mousse a l'orange*, followed by a special coffee that Anton favored. Lulled by the music, the good food, her companion's strangely respectful demeanor, Amber was not prepared for his next suggestion.

"Let's get out of here," he said abruptly, wiping his mouth and refolding the napkin. He rose, stretching out his hand as if expecting her to read his mind. "We have some business to attend to."

"B-but. . . ." As far as Amber knew, she had wound up all the loose ends at the office before she left. Her replacement knew how to access all files on current contracts, where to find supplies, how to contact her in Paris if anything came up. "Where are we going?"

"You'll see." He inserted a hundred-dollar bill in the leather folder Eddie had left on their table, came around, and took her firmly by the arm, steering her through the tables of diners still lingering over their meal or dancing to the haunting melody of "Blue Moon."

It was an oldie, but as the singer crooned the words into a microphone, the message was as new as tonight: "Blue moon, you left me standing alone. . .without a dream in my heart . . .without a love of my own." It followed her all the way to the car, onto the freeway, and up a familiar, winding road. She wondered if the words were somehow prophetic.

ॐ

When Amber stepped out of the Mercedes in front of Anton's estate, she shivered. The air was considerably cooler here, and the mist was rising above the cliffs, threatening to obscure the house and grounds. It was a lovely, eerie sight. Surreal. Much as the evening had been.

Anton was at her side in an instant, covering her bare shoulders with the wrap she had brought. "You're cold. Let's skip the beach and go inside."

"This shawl. . .it isn't mine, either, you know," she replied, stumbling over her explanation, as if to hold him at bay with words. "It belongs to the Pasetti Agency. Just as I do. . .for one more night. But after that, I won't be your secretary—"

Anton smiled. "Amber, Amber. . .don't fret. I'm not going to harm you. Just trust me."

Trust him? Now that's the last thing she would do. But she should hear him out. Maybe he really did have a little more business to discuss. Maybe it had something to do with her trip tomorrow.

He led her inside and up the stairs to his study, where they had talked once before. He struck a match and lit the fire that had already been laid, then lowered the lights. She sat down stiffly on a chair, putting as much distance between them as the room would allow.

Anton took off his tuxedo jacket and threw it over the back of the couch. "Now that you're leaving, I think it's time we were honest with each other."

He wanted to be honest? The biggest con artist of all time? She felt her eyes widen. Her lashes grazed the hair falling over her face, and she pushed the strands back over one ear, no longer concerned about her appearance.

"I have an idea that you've been able to put your fiancé's death behind you while you've been with us. . .that you're no longer grieving. Am I right?"

She nodded slowly.

"You no longer love him." It was a statement, not a question.

"I really don't see what business it is of yours. . . ." The look on his face silenced her, and she shook her head.

Anton rose and paced in front of the fire. Then he turned to face her. "I'll have to admit I had other plans for us tonight. Oh, you would have resisted, but I intended to pull out all the stops." He looked deep into her eyes. "But there is something about you tonight, something I can't put my finger on. . .that changed my mind."

Amber let out her breath in a soundless sigh, unaware that she'd been holding it. *Thank You, Lord.*

"Still, I'd like. . .I *need* to tell you about. . .Layla."

She leaned back against her chair, watching the strong

line of his jaw flex and relax. What more could he tell her than she already knew? Charis and Len had confided in her from the first about the sad loss of their only daughter. She even knew that Anton and Layla had planned to marry.

He dropped down onto the couch and stared into the fire. "She was young and beautiful. . .and driven." It seemed to Amber that at that moment, the years fell away and he was in the past—with Layla. "I was in my early twenties; she was nineteen. We were," he paused, searching for the right words, "very close. We were both enamored of ourselves, the glamour, the possibilities for success. We felt nothing could stand in our way. Mother was running the business then. . . ."

There was a long pause while he contemplated the fire. Then he rose, drove his hands into his pants pockets, and hunched his shoulders. Standing there like that, he looked young and vulnerable. Amber's heart went out to him. "She *used* me. . .used me to buy herself a contract from my mother, to make a place for herself in the business! And I fell for it."

He sighed, long and deep. "Oh, Layla came back to me. . . between jobs. . .when she wasn't doing some movie or TV commercial—bit parts mostly. She had everything: beauty, guts, determination. She could have made it on her own. . . but she chose to take a shortcut." The memory seemed overwhelming. "Or maybe she just *enjoyed* playing around, wielding her power over men." He let out a bitter laugh.

"We aren't sure if her drug overdose was accidental, or if it was because she finally saw the futility of it all. A film producer she had decided to marry jilted her, and she didn't get the contract she was after."

Drug overdose? Amber was stunned. Len and Charis hadn't shared that part of the story. "I'm sorry, Anton. . . so sorry. You must have loved her very much."

"No, I didn't love her," he blurted, with such a tortured look on his face that Amber shivered in spite of the warmth of the fire. "I don't think either of us was mature enough for real love. But her death was a blow to me. For several years afterward, I spent a lot of time abroad, handling our businesses in Paris and London. Then Mother got sick."

Amber didn't think she could stand much more. Seeing Anton like this. . .

But he went on. "The next few years made me face up to my responsibility, take over the reins. I've tried to run the business as I think Mother would have run it." Tears glimmered in the silvery eyes. "Because of her—her standards, her values—I try to be as honest with others as I expect them to be with me."

I know what he's going to say now, Amber thought. Hoping to shut out the imagined sound of those words, she cleared her throat. She'd say it for him and get it over with. "You're in love with Gina."

His harsh laugh was a jolt. "Gina and I are. . .honest with each other," he began, neither admitting nor denying what Amber had said. "I have some. . .plans for her. But I'd never tell a woman I loved her if I didn't mean it."

He hurried on. "Gina makes no pretense about what she wants, either. . .personal or professional. And I make no pretense in letting her, or anyone else, know they can advance with my agency only if they please my clients. There are no contracts based on one's. . .compatibility. . . with the owner of the company."

It took a while for the words to sink in. Then Amber felt the color storm to her face. "You *still* think I. . . ?"

She jumped to her feet and walked over to the heavy scarlet draperies covering the sliding glass doors to the balcony. Parting them, she saw her own reflection in the glass. With her hair falling over her face again, she looked like a stranger, the gray mist outside swirling around her image. Maybe it was all a dream. . .a nightmare! She'd surely wake up and find that none of this had happened.

"I'm not blaming you, Amber," he said amiably. "I understand completely. I believe you're a true innocent. . . pure, untouched. And I'm enough of a gentleman to leave that alone. I'm simply offering you some sound advice that could save you a lot of trouble in the future. . .particularly in Paris. I'm trying to say that my experiences with women like Layla and Gina have taught me how important career advancement can be to a woman. It won't work with me. . .not anymore. But some men wouldn't hesitate to take advantage of you."

Amber was mortified! How could she have had feelings for this impossible man who never believed a word she said? He had his own mind made up that all women were devious, and nothing she could say ever seemed to dent that stubborn insistence.

"I just want you to know, Amber, that if you have your heart set on modeling—as a permanent career— Pasetti Agency will back you and work for you. I'll hire another secretary, and we'll issue a long-term modeling contract. . . ."

He was still talking. Would he never stop? "When you get back, I'd be willing to escort you to places like the one we visited tonight—places our clients frequent—so they can get a look at you. I have no doubt you'll be a very successful model for Pasetti Agency. That innocent look will take you a long way. It'll be a refreshing new slant on selling in an industry that's seen everything else. I'm afraid we're all pretty jaded by now."

When she didn't reply, he kept on. "I know how much you enjoyed tonight," he said. "The glamour of it, the clothes, the attention. You seemed to light up. That mysterious sadness was gone. In fact, tonight you were a very different person, all aglow, lovely."

He didn't understand. Would *never* understand. Her head whirled like the mist outside. She couldn't hear any more. She didn't belong here. She had to get away. Back to the cottage. Back to the real world. "Please. . .take me home. I have some more packing to do."

He frowned. She could see his jaw clench again. "Very well. Anything you say." He was all business again. "I had hoped we could come to terms. . .but apparently you aren't ready to open up to me." He narrowed his gaze sharply. "Just keep in mind what I've told you. The offer stands."

She jumped up and got her wrap before he could reach her, then prceded him down the stairs and out the massive front doorway. Mitchell was nowhere in sight. No doubt Anton had briefed the staff ahead of time.

The mist clung to her face, mingling with the tears that were beginning to trickle down her cheeks. She braced herself. *No time for that, Amber. As Aunt Sophie would say, 'The Lord never closes a door that He doesn't open a window.'* Apparently Anton was a closed door. No, make that a *slammed* door. He didn't even understand the basic reasons for the differences between them. She'd just have to keep looking for that open window. . .and praying for Anton's soul.

Neither of them spoke all the way back to the cottage. The car moved swiftly through the murky night, making hazy circles in the fog. The full moon that had been clearly visible earlier was hidden from view. Just like so many things about her life, Amber thought.

She tried not to notice when Anton did not take her arm as they walked across her backyard. Nor did he ask for her key, but let her fumble with the lock herself. He waited, rigidly, near the door as she made a hasty inspection and returned to give him the all-clear.

But he seemed reluctant to leave. "I hope you won't allow anything I've said tonight to harm our working relationship. You're a very valuable employee, Amber. . .more now than ever."

She shook her head. Of *course* she was more valuable. Models brought in more dollars for the agency than mere secretaries. The flood that had been threatening to break loose was just behind her eyelids.

"You'll be all right?"

"Of course," she answered, not daring to look at him, hoping he'd leave before she made an idiot of herself.

He stepped back and, with his hand on the doorknob, turned once more. "Have a safe flight. . .and may God go with you. . . and keep you safe."

That was all it took. The minute he was out the door, the dam broke, and she leaned back against the door and released all the tears she'd been holding back.

"Lord, why? Why does it have to end this way?"

fourteen

Red roses were waiting in Amber's plush hotel room when she arrived on Monday afternoon, Paris time. The card read simply: "All good wishes, Anton." This time the long-stemmed beauties marked the beginning of a truly new career, if she decided she wanted it, and the end of a relationship that was over before it had begun.

She was too tired to register any emotion. The famous jet lag she'd heard so much about, probably. Not only that, but she was still drained from her last painful encounter with Anton.

On the plane, she had had time to do a lot of thinking and praying. It seemed symbolic somehow that she was running away from yet another heartache—this time with *wings*. Still, the distance would give her some space to gain perspective on the whole thing. And God was still in control. . .even if He sometimes seemed to operate on a different timetable.

She unpacked her Bible and set it on the dainty nightstand. Knowing absolutely no one in the city, there would be plenty of time to read. Maybe she could find some guidance for the future. . .when all this was over and she was back home in North Carolina.

The jangle of the telephone jarred her from her thoughts. Who could that be? Someone back at the office must be needing something. For a moment she found herself hoping it was Anton, checking to see if she'd had a safe flight.

Shaking off the memory of his mellow baritone, she lifted the receiver. "Hello. Amber Jennings."

A familiar masculine voice greeted her.

"Ron? Ron Jordan? Is that you? What's wrong? Something at the office? Did I leave—" Rattled, she broke off to catch her breath.

"Hey, hold it! Nothing's wrong. And I'm not at the office. I'm here. . .right here in Paris."

"Here? In Paris?" she squeaked.

"In the same hotel. . .Room 412. I arrived yesterday. So I'm all over my jet lag and ready to show you the enchanted city."

Amber's brain felt numb. "But, Ron, what are you *doing* here?"

"Same thing you are. The 'Innocence in Paris' shoot. Anton thought I'd be great as your male counterpart. My blond looks, your brunette beauty. You know, wholesome, clean-cut guy meets girl next door. Nostalgia's in. . .or had you forgotten?"

She reached for her briefcase and pulled out the fax Anton had given her just before she left and scanned it again:

> *Anton, your Amber Jennings is perfect for our "Innocence in Paris" collection. We must contract for her immediately. She has that fresh, innocent appeal we're looking for. Every woman in the world will want to look just like her. Once again, you've proven to be a genius, dear boy. Fly her to us!*

Amber had been stunned. *His Amber Jennings!* How could Anton have pretended to resent her posing for Len, then use those very photos to "sell" her to some client—and without even asking her permission?! She was still furious with him.

"Amber, are you there?"

"What? Oh, yes. Sorry, Ron. I'm still in the clouds, I think."

"Well, why don't you take a nap, then put on one of those knockout dresses Charis lined up for you, and let's go out for a late dinner."

"Sure," she replied noncommittally. "Sounds good. I'll give you a buzz when I wake up."

Amber kicked off her shoes and finished her unpacking, hanging the clothes in the full closet and putting away the undergarments and makeup, all courtesy of the Pasetti Agency. Not a scrap of clothing and none of the accessories she'd brought belonged to her. Even from a distance, Anton still controlled her. And now, he'd sent Ron. She wouldn't be surprised if that had been planned by the boss, too, simply to keep an eye on her!

Speaking of eyes, she ought to check on her bruise before she went out in public. The "Veronica Lake look" was beginning to be a nuisance.

In the bathroom, she was startled to find an unusual piece of porcelain plumbing. She'd have to ask about that. Leaning over to look in the gilded mirror over the basin, she examined her eye. The bruise was fading nicely. But she could definitely use some sleep. She washed her face, then padded back to the bedroom in her stocking feet.

Plumping the pillows, she pulled back the brocade

bedspread and lay down. She was asleep almost before her head hit the pillow, her last troubled thoughts of Anton.

❧

"We've missed April in Paris," Ron quipped when he came by her room to pick her up for dinner, "but May isn't half bad. There are flowers everywhere." Spotting the roses in the tall vase on the *écritoire,* he grinned. "I see you already have a sample."

She smiled, but didn't explain, and turned to lock the door behind her.

When she turned around, Ron was standing very near. "You're gorgeous tonight, Amber. Love your new hairstyle. And that dress—wow! Green is my favorite color, you know."

She glanced up to see if he was kidding. "Ron. . .it's *blue*. . .periwinkle, to be exact."

He shrugged and grinned. "Oh. . .did I also tell you I'm color blind?"

In spite of her exhaustion and her preoccupation with Anton, Amber giggled. "Where are we going for dinner?"

"Surprise," Ron said, leading the way to the elevator at the end of the corridor. "It isn't Maxim's, but Anton said you'd love it. Said he wanted your first night in Paris to be spectacular. So just relax and enjoy the ride."

Puzzled, she followed him into the elevator. When she had first arrived at the Richelieu, she had been too tired to notice much about her surroundings. But now she took in the splendor—French furnishings complete with elegant gold leaf, ornate mirrors, and massive arrangements of fresh flowers adorning every available surface in the lobby.

Outside, Ron carried on a brief conversation with the liveried doorman, and a limousine drove up.

"How did you manage that?" Amber wanted to know. "I didn't know you spoke French."

He patted his coat. "Handy vest-pocket dictionary. But I didn't order a limo, I asked for a taxi. Must have been Pasetti's idea." He frowned a little, then shrugged. "Oh, well. We might as well travel in style; he can afford it. My French might have gotten us *to* the restaurant, but after that. . . ." He spread his hands.

Feeling more lighthearted than she had felt in quite some time, Amber laughed as he settled her in the back seat of the limo and ran around to slide in beside her. She still couldn't believe she was in Paris! From a small town North Carolina to the streets of the world's most romantic city in only a few months! She ignored the twinge of regret that she wasn't here with someone more special than good old Ron.

Leaning forward to take in the sights as the driver made his way through the crowded streets, Amber could see that the city sparkled. No wonder Paris was known as "The City of Lights." It practically vibrated with life and motion. There were people everywhere—windowshopping along the wide boulevards, sitting at sidewalk cafés, strolling in one of the fabulous gardens they passed. The sight of a couple openly embracing near one of the fountains brought back another scene—Anton's rooftop garden. Could she never escape the thought of him?

"We'll have plenty of time to do some sightseeing in the next few days," Ron was saying. "Our first fitting is not until day after tomorrow, although Madame Collette wants to meet us at two. She promised we'd be through by three, and the shoot doesn't start until next week. So. . . *ma chérie*," he leered playfully, twirling a make-believe moustache, "I will haff you all to myself. I will not let you out of my sight. I will be your personal tour guide. Trust me."

She couldn't help laughing. "And I'm to trust *your* French?" With a shock of hair falling over one eye and that fake accent, he seemed more like Peter Sellers in one of those old "Pink Panther" movies. "Sorry, Ron," she said. "You'd be more believable as a Swiss ski instructor."

They were still laughing when the driver pulled over to the curb in front of a quaint building with an awning extending over the sidewalk. A doorman sprang to open the door. *"Bon soir, monsieur, mademoiselle."*

Amber took his hand and stepped out, feeling like a celebrity. Apparently Anton hadn't spared any expense. But he'd do the same for any of his models. Didn't Gina always have the best? And when Ron mumbled another phrase in French, the only word she could make out was *"Pasetti"*

They didn't need the dictionary for the rest of the evening. Apparently the Pasetti name was the key that unlocked all the golden doors. Inside the restaurant, they were shown to a corner table, where three uniformed waiters appeared instantly. One was holding a bouquet of red roses, which he presented to Amber; another trundled over an iced bucket of—not champagne, but Perrier; still another produced a large menu, then spoke in startlingly flawless English, "If I may be so bold, may I recommend the speciality of the house: filets de sole Cardinal and scallop salad with truffles?"

Amber and Ron looked at each other and gave a helpless shrug. "Bring it on," Ron ordered.

The rest of the evening proceeded without a hitch. It was as if Anton himself were orchestrating the entire event and was standing by, somewhere in the shadows, to be sure they had the best of everything. Amber could almost feel his presence. Still, when she glanced up occasionally to look through the window, it wasn't *two* dark heads reflected there, but Ron's blond one beside hers.

Noticing her sudden silence, he spoke up. "You do recognize those tall spires over there, don't you? That's the Notre Dame Cathedral located on the Ile de la Cité. I think that's why Anton chose this particular restaurant. He knew you'd like—" He broke off as if disgusted with himself, and speared a forkful of sole. "We'll have lots of time to explore the city. Besides," he cocked his head, grinning at her, "I have another surprise for you. . .something you're *really* not going to believe!"

Later, at a little sidewalk bistro, when they met up with Kate and Jim, Amber was stunned. "What are you two doing over here?"

After hugs, Kate gave a sheepish grin. "I was going to tell you, Amber, really I was. . .but everything happened so fast. . .and you were so busy getting ready for your shoot. . .and," the words tumbling out rose to a shriek, "Jim and I are *married!*"

Amber could only gasp. "*Married?* But when. . . ?"

"Day before yesterday. I'll tell you all about it later. It was just that Daddy was suddenly transferred to another base, and the wedding had to be rushed up, or you *know* you would have been my maid of honor. As it turned out, it was just a simple ceremony with only the family. But, Amber, the best part—"

"Let *me* tell her." Jim, who had been standing by quietly, broke in. "Mr. Pasetti is giving us this honeymoon trip. . .so we could be here to help out with the cosmetic shoot week after next." His grin shifted to a stern scowl. "But let me warn you. We plan to make ourselves scarce until we're actually needed. After all, this *is* our honeymoon."

"Hey, pal, congratulations!" Ron clapped his friend on the back. "This is news to me, too. But don't worry, we aren't likely to be running into you. It's a big city, and we have a few plans of our own."

There was lots of laughter and catching up over *café au lait*. From the corner of her eye, Amber could see the amused smiles of passersby, overhearing their chatter. To them, it must appear that the two couples were rendezvousing, both pairs giddy with the excitement of being in love.

She took a moment to watch Ron as he filled their friends in on their schedule for the next two weeks. He *was* extremely attractive—those perfect, even features, his face so animated as he talked. Still, as Aunt Sophie had often said, "I hear married folks say it's not looks that counts . . .though it doesn't hurt any to get yourself a good-lookin' one. No, the man you marry better be your best friend, someone who can make you laugh, 'cause you're going to be spending an awful lot of time together!"

Well, Amber hadn't had a better friend than Ron. . .not

since Ken. Ron kept her in stitches. She hadn't laughed so much in ages.

"So," he was telling Jim and Kate as Amber shook off her thoughts, "we'll stay out of *your* way if you'll stay out of *ours*."

Now, what did he mean by that?

"Hey, wife," Jim said, helping Kate up, "it's one o'clock in the morning. We're still trying to adjust to Paris time, you know—"

"And Amber needs her beauty sleep," Ron added, then amended, "What I mean is, she's exhausted from her trip, and tomorrow is a big day. So. . .we'll say *adieu*," he scrambled for his pocket dictionary, "or is it *au revoir?*"

Kate giggled, and Amber got to her feet, suddenly overwhelmed with all that had happened in the past few days. "Ron's right. I *do* need my beauty sleep. I'm still fighting some swelling in this eye." She touched the area where makeup had concealed most of the fading bruise. "I don't need bags, too!"

With another round of laughter and the promise to get together at the first shoot, Ron hailed a cab. All the way back to the hotel, he joked about the surprise wedding and their unpredictable friends.

At her door, he made a mock bow and kissed his fingers. "*Mademoiselle,* Paree is *nossing* compared to your beauty. I would like to book every available moment of your time while we are here, *s'il vous plait.*"

When he straightened, though, there was no trace of levity in his expression. "I mean it, Amber. I'd like the chance to let you see that I'm not just some goofy guy with a crush on the latest Pasetti star." He flexed his jaw.

"Tonight might have been compliments of the great Anton Pasetti. . .but the rest is on me. I want us to get to know each other better on this trip. . .*much* better."

His eyes held hers in a steady gaze, and she couldn't look away. "I'd like that, too," she whispered before unlocking the door and stepping aside.

Long after she was in bed, her mind churned. Maybe this was what it was all about. Maybe this was why she had come halfway across the country—to San Diego—and now halfway across the world. She and Ron. Was he God's best for her?

≈

The next week passed in a blur. Anton had arranged a session at Carita, one of the city's finest beauty salons, for a facial, manicure and pedicure, and hair styling. For the fashion shoot, it was decided that Amber's eye had sufficiently healed to wear her hair pulled off her face in a fresh, natural style. *"Très ingénue, mademoiselle. Très naturelle,"* the stylist murmured. "Makes the eyes appear wide and vulnerable, *non?"*

From there, Amber was introduced to Madame Collette, the couturière who had designed the line of clothing she would be modeling.

"Très belle!" Madame exclaimed the minute she saw Amber, which Amber correctly translated, "Beautiful!" But when the woman, a tiny wisp of a thing with hair piled on top of her head, exploded in a volley of French phrases, Amber lost her. From the smiles of the staff looking on, she assumed they were pleased.

"Enchanting, *ma chérie,"* Madame said in passable English. "So right for my collection. Our Paris models in the *haute couture* houses have the. . .what shall we say? . . .the seductive look. But you. . .there is such innocence . . .such purity. *Mais oui,* I know what it is. . .it is the look of a Botticelli angel!"

There were long afternoons and evenings with Ron, too. Times when they could get away to take in all the city had to offer. Since both were on an expense account and wanted to be fair to the agency, they used a cab for only those attractions that were not within walking distance. They browsed through the stalls of the booksellers, strolled the Luxembourg Gardens, ate lunch in a bistro beneath the Eiffel Tower.

At one of the boutiques, Ron insisted on buying her a vial of real perfume, *L'Heure Bleue,* "for women who are romantic, sensitive, refined, and feminine." She brushed it on the pulsepoint at her wrist, and he lifted her arm to sniff, then dropped a kiss on the spot.

I'm beginning to like this guy, she admitted to herself. More than she would have believed possible. More than she had intended.

&

On Sunday morning, Amber found Ron waiting for her in the lobby. "I know we didn't discuss this last night, and I hope you don't mind," he began on an apologetic note, "but I knew you'd probably be looking for a place to worship. Right?"

She blushed, and didn't know why. Her faith was very important to her, and almost everyone back at the agency knew it. "Yes. I'd planned to take a cab to one of the churches. We haven't visited any yet and. . .well, today seemed like the right time."

"Then, allow me. I have an idea I know just the place."
He offered her his arm, stepped confidently through the
front doorway, and ordered a taxi in fluent French.

"I'm impressed. You've been practicing."

"Just the most important phrases," he gave her a searching look, "but I'm saving some of those for later."

She wasn't surprised when the driver crossed one of
the many bridges leading to Notre Dame Cathedral. Amber
hadn't had such a grand place in mind. She'd been hoping
for a smaller, more intimate place, where she could drop
into a back pew and pray quietly while the Parisians wor-
shipped. But this was thoughtful of Ron, who was obviously making a noble effort to do the right thing.

Inside the great Gothic building with its twin towers, there
was a steady stream of spectators. The two rose windows, dating back to the 13th century, were magnificent,
and remarkable sculptures depicted Christ at the Last Judg-
ment and other sacred works. It was all very interesting,
but the vast interior was cold and impersonal. Amber felt
separated from God rather than closer to Him. In fact, it
seemed dark and oppressive in here, she thought, and she
was eager to get back out into the sunshine.

But before she stepped through the door leading outside, Ron pulled her into a secluded corner of the cathedral. "There's something I need to tell you, Amber."

This wasn't the fun-loving man she'd come to know.
This was a much more serious Ron.

"I've been a Christian since I was a boy," he shuffled
his feet, looking down, "but I must admit it's been a long
time since I've put my faith into action...like you seem to
do without thinking about it twice. Until you invited me to

church at the beach, I hadn't darkened the door since. . . well, that's another story. It's not the politically correct thing to do in this industry, you know." He looked up, gazing at her intently. "But it's different now. You've helped me see what's really important. . .no matter what people might think."

Amber nodded, feeling she had no right to be hearing Ron's confession. This was too personal; it was something that should be shared only with the woman. . . . It was all moving too fast. . .much too fast. She didn't want to hear any more. But he wasn't through.

"*Je t'aime.* Translation, in case you haven't been doing your homework, I think I'm falling in love with you, Amber."

Until this moment she had thought she had put Anton completely out of her mind, out of her heart. But it was no use. Why couldn't *he* be here, saying these words? "Not now, Ron. This isn't the time. Please, could we go? It's chilly in here."

She had prayed for Anton Pasetti every day. But she hadn't counted on loving him so much it hurt.

fifteen

It was just as Gina had said.

Modeling was hard work. Long hours under the hot lights. Holding a pose when your back was aching. Looking into Ron's blue eyes when it was Anton's dark gray ones Amber was seeing. It was all she could do to keep that fresh-faced glow when her spirits were about as low as they had ever been.

She had never prayed so hard in her life. Just about the time she'd thought she was beginning to make some sense of everything that had happened, she'd discovered that she was her own worst enemy! That Anton had never been far from her thoughts. And that she could never love Ron in the same way. Was she rebelling against all the Lord wanted for her? She'd tried to let it go, but the more she prayed for Anton, the more her thoughts and feelings followed.

Still, *something* was working. At least, Madame Collette was pleased. "She has zee face of an angel," she would say to anyone who would listen.

Amber was always embarrassed by the woman's remarks, but when she would blush, Madame would emote even more. "Do you see? How pure. . .how untouched she is! Most women today haff forgotten how to blush."

The "Innocence in Paris" line was a sensation. At several fashion shows Amber modeled the latest day and evening attire for the "wholesome, natural girl" and swimwear for "the innocent." The results of the grueling photo sessions appeared in the Parisian papers, calling her "a stunning new find."

Amber was relieved when the fashion shoot was over. That meant Ron would be returning to San Diego soon. Not that he'd given up on her. That day in the cathedral, when she hadn't been able to hide the truth, she'd seen the pain in his eyes.

But he had rebounded quickly. And by morning, he was at her door with a rose between his teeth, begging her to give him another chance. "*Je, t'adore*, Amber. You are zee only woman in my life!"

She hadn't wanted to hurt him, but she'd had to tell him she wasn't ready to make a commitment. It had been painful for them both. So Charis and Len's arrival the following week was a welcome reprieve.

Madame Collette repeated her sentiments to the Lamarrs. "She is all yours. . .at least for zee moment," Madame said with a secretive smile. "But I haff zee plan . . .I shall fax Anton and we shall discuss it."

When Kate and Jim showed up to assist with the shoot, Kate was ecstatic. "Oh, Amber, Paris is the most perfect place for a honeymoon. We'll never forget it, will we, darling?" She looked at her new husband as if he were a chocolate éclair, and she could easily devour him in one mouthful. Lucky Kate.

Amber had to fight back a feeling of jealousy. She was probably destined to be alone for the rest of her life. Even her aunt, who had responded to her postcards, was on the verge of "taking the leap after all these years." Lucky

Aunt Sophie.

With Kate and Jim assisting Charis, Len's shoot went well. But about the only positive thing Amber could find was that the "haunting" look they needed for the "Woman of Mystery" line could be called up at a moment's notice. All she had to do was think of Anton, and the photographer got exactly the shot he was after.

Because of the chemistry that was flowing, the shoot took practically no time at all, much to the delight of everyone concerned. Kate and Jim were eager to get back to San Diego and begin their new life as husband and wife. Len and Charis had important business to attend to.

"I really can't be away from the office another day," Charis confided. "Amber, darling, you must know how very pleased we are with your work. Your professionalism has saved us a great deal of time and money."

"Yeah, but there goes my tennis partner," Len cracked. "She'll be so much in demand now that we'll never see her."

Just as they were packing up the equipment to be shipped back to the States, Madame Collette appeared on the set with the look of a cat eyeing a bowl of cream. "Ah, *chérie,* there you are! It appears dear Anton has released you to me. . .just as I had hoped."

Amber was shocked. "W-what?"

"You are my inspiration! I must have you near me to complete another line of designs. Zey will be a masterpiece—the *pièce de résistance*—the crowning achievement of a lifetime! I will call it—'Angelique'!"

Len and Charis were equally stunned. "What are you talking about, Collette?" Len demanded, instantly defensive. "Amber has a contract as a Pasetti model. And, more than that, she has a life of her own to consider. How could Anton do a thing like this without consulting her?"

Madame Collette smiled. "Oh, don't fret, *mon ami,* I shall do what is right by her. I shall pay her much more than she would receive anywhere else in zee world! Besides, with my 'angel' to inspire me, I shall complete zee line quickly. . . say no more than seex months."

"Six months!" The three dropped their mouths.

"She shall have zee best accommodations and plenty of time to enjoy our beautiful city, *non?* What woman would not love such an arrangement, eh?"

Suddenly everything seemed clear to Amber. There was no place for her back home. Her best friend was married now. Aunt Sophie and Uncle Jack would probably follow suit pretty soon. And Anton had let her go—without so much as asking her opinion! No secretarial job. No modeling contract. What did she have to go back to?

Before Charis or Len could object further, Amber spoke up. "I accept, Madame Collette. When do you want me to begin?"

❧

Amber wasn't quite sure how Aunt Sophie would take the news that she was going to stay on in Paris. Her aunt hadn't been too keen about it in the first place. "I've heard that city is full of all kinds of sin and perversions," she'd warned. "Just don't forget your upbringing." But now that she had Uncle Jack to think about, she hadn't corresponded lately.

Kate was delighted. "Aren't you the lucky one?" she wrote. "Now you'll get to see all the places you missed. Kick back, friend, and enjoy. You deserve it!

"As for Jim and me, we're more in love every day. We're planning to celebrate our first anniversary in Paris—at the same small hotel where we spent our honeymoon. It's quaint, charming, and well off the main thoroughfares. You might want to check it out. If so, be sure to give the proprietors, Monsieur and Madame LaRue, our love. They're such dears."

With Kate's directions, the place wasn't hard to find, and Amber soon moved out of the Richelieu and settled into her new routine. The LaRues were everything Kate had said they were, and more, a French version of Aunt Sophie and Uncle Jack. She felt right at home.

She was expected at Madame Collette's shop for only a couple of hours a day to sit for sketches. Later, as the garments were developed, she would have to be measured and fitted once again. For now, most of her days were free to absorb the ambiance of the city. If she was lucky, she might even be able to put Anton out of her mind once and for all.

But no matter where she went—shopping in the boutiques that lined the wide avenues, spending an afternoon in one of the famous museums, stopping for croissants and *café au lait* at one of the sidewalk bistros—it took only a glimpse of a strong profile or a dark head to bring the images flashing back.

There was an occasional letter from Ron. "Just to remind you that I'm still around, waiting for you back in sunny California. Be good. . .and remember—*je t'aime.*"

❧

Soon after becoming a resident of the little hotel, Amber discovered a chapel nearby. It was centuries old and covered with ivy, but the interior had been restored back during the War, she learned, and a few people from the neighborhood, most of them elderly Parisians, had volunteered to clip back the weeds and clean the vestry, then gathered to pray from time to time.

As the season subtly shifted to autumn and the leaves turned, she began to drop by more and more frequently to soak in the peace and to pray for guidance. When Madame Collette's collection was finished, Amber hadn't the slightest idea of what she would do. Always, though, after coming here to the chapel, she left with a sense that God was working out the details of her life. . .if she only had patience to wait on Him.

And always, always, she prayed for Anton. If she could do nothing else, she could ask God to protect him, to make him happy with Gina, to heal his heart and save him from his own foolishness.

૨૦

By the end of November, Madame Collette was putting the finishing touches on her new collection. "Ah, this is my best work. I shall have a. . .how you say? . . .a preliminary showing—with you as zee only model, of course. We shall begin with a little reception in my salon for only my best customairs and their daughters, home for the holidays. They will see you in my enchanting designs. . .and beg their *mamans* for a new frock. And you, *chérie,* will be dazzling in *blanc!*"

"*Blanc?* White?"

Madame beamed. "Yes—*blanc,* ivory, *crème.* And now you know my secret." Her pale eyes danced. "All the garments in this collection will be white—velvets, wools,

satins. White. . .like the snow! Ah, I can see it now!"
She clasped her hands together. "In the midst of winter's
bleakness. . .the light! *Perfection! Brillant!* Even *I* have
never been so inspired." She laughed with delight and
gazed at Amber fondly. "It is you, Angelique, who inspire
me."

❧

On the afternoon of the showing, after the final presenta-
tion—a magnificent bridal creation in satin and lace—
Amber headed for the dressing room to change. She was
exhausted. She'd made eight changes: a silk gown and
peignor set; loungewear in brushed velvet; a worsted wool
skirt and cashmere turtleneck, worn with high-heeled kid
boots. . .ending with Madame Collette's masterpiece.

She lifted the long satin skirt and hurried into the room.
The sooner she got out of this heavy dress, the better.

At the dressing table, she removed the tiara and veil and
was pulling out the pins in her upswept hairdo when she
heard a knock at the door. "*Entrez-vous, Madame.*"

But it wasn't Madame Collette. Amber's eyes locked
with a familiar pair of smoky gray ones. "Anton!"

"Put on something warm. I have a car waiting."

She came up out of her seat and turned to face him.
"Just a minute! How dare you show up after all this time
and start ordering me around! I'm not your secretary.
I'm not a Pasetti model. I'm not on your payroll at all,"
she hesitated at the smile tugging at his lower lip, "or am
I? Have you and Madame Collette been conspiring behind my back?"

His silence spoke louder than words before he went on.
"Ah, Amber, I'm relieved to see that you haven't changed

at all. You still look glorious when you're all heated up like that." His gaze swept the wedding gown. "You always did go in for those high-necked affairs, didn't you? All right, all right," he backed off, seeing the fire in her eyes. "I'll rephrase my invitation. When you've changed, would you do me the honor of accompanying me to dinner? There is a matter of some. . .urgent business that must be handled . . .and only you have the answer."

She sighed, skeptical. She'd been expecting something like this. No doubt the new secretary hadn't been able to locate a file or a contract. "I should have my head examined. . .but I'll go. Give me a minute."

"Just remember," he grinned, flashing white teeth, "I'm not a patient man."

Hurrying back into the wool outfit and boots, Amber grabbed a hooded ivory greatcoat and joined him in the salon. Without another word, he led her outside to a sleek, low-slung car at the curb. A few flakes of snow drifted out of the sky, and their breath frosted in the cold air.

They passed now-familiar sights, but nothing registered. Only the man seated beside her in the little sports car filled her senses. He was so close she could touch him, yet he was completely beyond her reach.

He turned in at a French café. "It's small, but the food here is excellent. I doubted that you would eat before the showing."

She nodded, not trusting herself to say a word.

They ate their meal in silence. The food, delicious as it might have been, tasted like sawdust in her mouth. Over coffee, Anton spoke softly, kindly, allowing her time to unwind, briefing her on office happenings in her absence, painting pictures in broad strokes. There was one major omission. Gina. What about Gina?

He sighed. "I have another offer," he said. "Another contract."

"Really? I'm sure Gina would be available." Amber couldn't resist the dig. "That is, unless she's too busy with her duties at home."

"At home? I wouldn't know anything about that. She's currently in New York, making the first of three movies. Her contract reads that she'll be tied up for the next five years. Seems she's wanted to act all along."

Amber couldn't stifle a gasp. "But I thought. . . ."

He shrugged. "I suppose I know what you must have been thinking. You despise me, don't you, Amber?"

The expression in Anton's eyes broke her heart. But she had to be firm. Even without Gina in the picture, they were worlds apart. "I don't despise you, Anton. But I think I understand you. Business always comes first, then pleasure. After that, everything—and everyone—else. I believe that's really why you never married."

He looked down at his cup, tracing the rim with his finger. "You're right about so many things. . .but not everything. When I was younger, I was too busy pursuing pleasure. Then there was Mother's illness, and afterward . . .I was too busy trying to keep the company going. After Layla. . .well, for so long there was no one who came close to capturing my heart for more than a short time. And, strange as it may seem to you," he looked up and the dark eyes shimmered silver in the candlelight, "I've always believed that marriage should be a lifetime agreement, don't you, Amber?"

When she didn't answer, he added, "You do believe it. That's why you couldn't go through with the marriage to Ken. . .or Ron." He smiled when she looked up in surprise. "Knowing you as I do, I don't think you'd ever agree to marry a man unless you loved him completely."

Amber's head whirled. The guillotine operators didn't have anything on this guy. In fact, being beheaded would be far easier than having to sit here and listen to this. She wondered what satisfaction he could possibly derive from torturing her.

"And now that your obligations to the Pasetti Agency—and Madame Collette—have come to an end, I want to offer you a contract I hope you won't refuse. I promise it will bring you everything the agency and I personally have to offer. It's a marriage contract, Amber. Can you forgive me for hurting you? For being a world-class jerk?"

"Wh-what?" She couldn't believe her ears. "I don't understand. You don't love me, Anton. And even if you do, I can't—"

She could not bear the humiliation. From somewhere inside her, anger and hurt surged up. "You can't run my life for me. I'm through with the Pasetti Agency. I'm through with *you.* Love and marriage are far more than a piece of paper! But you wouldn't understand anything about *that!*"

He smiled sadly. "Of course I love you, Amber. I've loved you ever since the day you came to my office, looking like a scared little rabbit, but so determined to make a new start. I've loved you even when I was so angry with you I could have drawn and quartered you. . .or swept you off your feet with kisses and caresses." He paused, adoring her with his eyes. "I hardly dared believe that someone so lovely could be just as lovely on the inside. You seemed too good to be true. And, I must admit, the businessman in me was almost convinced, at times, that you were just another conniving female, jockeying for a career, but with a little different twist."

In spite of herself, Amber was fascinated. "I. . .I know how confusing that must be. Working with Madame Collette has taught me a great deal. And I've seen for myself that some people will do anything to get ahead."

"But there's more, Amber." He reached across the table and covered her hand with his own. "Since you've been away, I've made a commitment. . .to the Lord."

She jerked her hand away, blinded with tears and fury and indignation. "Now you really *have* gone too far with your games, with your pretending! And you almost had me believing that you. . . . How could you lie about something so important?!"

He shook his head. "Please. . .there's one more stop we need to make."

He didn't touch her, but allowed her to struggle into her coat and follow him out to the car. They drove through the crowded streets, taking several turns until they emerged into a quiet neighborhood, by now endearingly familiar. To Amber's amazement, he pulled the car to a stop in front of the ivy-covered chapel where she had spent so much time, shed so many tears.

He opened her door and she got out reluctantly. "I don't see what—"

He silenced her with an uplifted hand. "Just give me a chance to explain."

He led her inside the now-deserted building, illuminated by candles flickering in front of the altar. She knew the little chapel by heart, could have found her way in the dark. She sat down at the back, ran her hand over the pew, worn smooth with time.

The moon through the stained-glass windows filtered onto Anton's upturned face. "I've had so many doubts, so much anger in me. But I *wanted* to believe. . .that God could take my pain from me, could forgive all the terrible mistakes. . .sins I've committed. But this industry is full of people just like me. They spend their lives, their money creating an illusion."

He turned to gaze down at Amber. "Until you came along, I had little evidence that faith really changes anyone. . .that it works, that it's *real*."

Amber held her breath. Was this the indomitable Anton Pasetti—a man willing to confess his faults? Willing to ask God to change him?

"I know now that the only real world is the world where God makes all things new. My mother tried to teach me . . .bless her heart. Charis and Len tried, too. And then God sent *you*. I've been going to the mission church, Amber. . .looking for whatever it was that gave you the courage and faith to start over. I found it. . .or rather, I should say, I found *Him*. But it was you who opened up that whole new world to me."

There was a very long pause before Anton continued. "Well, now you know the whole truth. I don't blame you for turning down my marriage proposal. I'm not nearly good enough for you. But I could send you to Rome, where you might find some good man. And don't forget

Ron. He's waiting patiently back home in San Diego. As for me, I can understand why you could never trust me again. I've hurt you too much."

Amber rose to stand beside him in the aisle. Moonlight spilled over the pews, drenching them in a golden glow. "Yes, you did hurt me, Anton. . .but you had your reasons. God knew it was for the best. Otherwise, we might both have missed His best plan for us."

She saw the cool mask slip over his features again, and hurried to finish what her heart leaped to say. "I think God knew what had to happen to bring us together. . .for the rest of our lives."

Almost as if in disbelief, Anton studied her features. "Darling, are you saying what I think you're saying?"

"Oh, Anton," she whispered, snuggling in his embrace, where she belonged, "I love you and, more than anything else in this whole new world, I want to marry you."

He held her as if he were afraid she might vanish into the night, as if she were some priceless object in the Louvres. "Are you sure, darling? Very sure?"

She pulled away just enough to look up at him, and cocked her head. "About that lifetime contract. . .where do I sign?"

A Letter To Our Readers

Dear Reader:

In order that we might better contribute to your reading enjoyment, we would appreciate your taking a few minutes to respond to the following questions. When completed, please return to the following:

Rebecca Germany, Managing Editor
Heartsong Presents
P.O. Box 719
Uhrichsville, Ohio 44683

1. Did you enjoy reading *A Whole New World*?
   ❑ Very much. I would like to see more books
      by this author!
   ❑ Moderately
      I would have enjoyed it more if _____

   _____

2. Are you a member of **Heartsong Presents**? ❑Yes ❑No
   If no, where did you purchase this book? _____

   _____

3. What influenced your decision to purchase this
   book? (Check those that apply.)

   ❑ Cover   ❑ Back cover copy

   ❑ Title   ❑ Friends

   ❑ Publicity   ❑ Other_____

4. How would you rate, on a scale from 1 (poor) to 5
   (superior), the cover design? _____

5. On a scale from 1 (poor) to 10 (superior), please rate the following elements.

___Heroine   ___Plot

___Hero   ___Inspirational theme

___Setting   ___Secondary characters

6. What settings would you like to see covered in **Heartsong Presents** books?_____

_____

_____

7. What are some inspirational themes you would like to see treated in future books?_____

_____

_____

8. Would you be interested in reading other **Heartsong Presents** titles?   ❑ Yes   ❑ No

9. Please check your age range:
  ❑ Under 18   ❑ 18-24   ❑ 25-34
  ❑ 35-45   ❑ 46-55   ❑ Over 55

10. How many hours per week do you read? _____

Name _____

Occupation _____

Address _____

City_____ State_____ Zip_____

101
Ways to Say
"*I Love You*"

How do you say I love you? By sending love notes via overnight delivery. . .by watching the sunrise together. . . by calling in "well" and spending the day together. . .by sharing a candlelight dinner on the beach. . .by praying for the man or woman God has chosen just for you.

When you've found *the one*, you can't do without *one hundred and one ways* to tell them exactly how you feel. Priced to be the perfect subsitute for a birthday card or love note, this book fits neatly into a regular envelope. Buy a bunch and start giving today!

Specially Priced!
Buy 10 for only $9.97!
or 5 for only $4.97!

48 pages, Paperbound, 3½" x 5½"

·····Hearts♥ng·······

HEARTSONG PRESENTS TITLES AVAILABLE NOW:

·········· Presents ··········

Great Inspirational Romance at a Great Price!

Heartsong Presents books are inspirational romances in contemporary and historical settings, designed to give you an enjoyable, spirit-lifting reading experience. You can choose wonderfully written titles from some of today's best authors like Veda Boyd Jones, Yvonne Lehman, Tracie J. Peterson, Nancy N. Rue, and many others.

When ordering quantities less than twelve, above titles are $2.95 each.

Heartsong Presents
Love Stories Are Rated G!

That's for godly, gratifying, and of course, great! If you love a thrilling love story, but don't appreciate the sordidness of some popular paperback romances, **Heartsong Presents** is for you. In fact, **Heartsong Presents** is the *only inspirational romance book club*, the only one featuring love stories where Christian faith is the primary ingredient in a marriage relationship.

Sign up today to receive your first set of four, never before published Christian romances. Send no money now; you will receive a bill with the first shipment. You may cancel at any time without obligation, and if you aren't completely satisfied with any selection, you may return the books for an immediate refund!

Imagine. . .four new romances every four weeks—two historical, two contemporary—with men and women like you who long to meet the one God has chosen as the love of their lives. . .all for the low price of $9.97 postpaid.

To join, simply complete the coupon below and mail to the address provided. **Heartsong Presents** romances are rated G for another reason: They'll arrive *Godspeed!*